Barbara Unković is of Croatian and English descent and was born in New Zealand. She is the author of four published books and has achieved considerable success in the Frank O'Connor and International Book Awards as well as the Fish Publishing One Page Prize and Writer's Bill Board.

About the Artist

Colin Unković has been airbrush painting since the late 1970s and working as a fulltime artist since 2006.

Based in Northland, New Zealand, he is one of New Zealand's most skilled airbrush artists. His finely detailed contemporary artworks often feature very smooth transitions of colour, which give each of his works a unique feel or sense of mood. He is self-taught and has developed many special techniques that allow him to highlight the interplay of light and shadow that can give a transient form or a fleeting glimpse, an almost sculptural quality. Colin draws his inspiration from the natural forms of New Zealand, particularly the coast and from the effect that its unusual quality of light possesses.

"I consider myself to be extremely fortunate in that I don't have to look very far for inspiration or motivation for my work. My studio is nestled in the bush overlooking the Pacific Ocean and this alone provides me with an endless variety of nuances of light and colour. I sometimes think I am a bit spoiled for choice. The physical location of my studio also serves me in another way. It allows me to continue to develop my own particular style. We all tend to be effected by our surroundings and as an artist this often shows through in the end product. This is certainly true for me. Trying to capture the moods of our New Zealand coastline is, I find, a challenging and very pleasurable endeavour."

Colin aims to create paintings that bring pleasure to the eye and give a true sense of the subject while sometimes leaving enough latitude for individual interpretation as to allow the brain to engage and finish the story.

When Colin visited Croatia in 2008 he was inevitably attracted to the natural, unspoilt beauty of the island of Korčula. In New Zealand, the light tends to be clear and crisp, whereas Colin found the light in Croatia to be softer, as if it has had the rough edges knocked off, thus giving it an older, more time worn look. It became a natural progression for Colin to create the artwork for all of his sister's books, *Adriatic Blue*, *Weeds in the Garden of Eden* and *Moon Walking*.

Colin's paintings hang in collections in New Zealand, the UK, the USA and Europe.

His website is www.colinunkovich.com

WEEDS IN THE GARDEN OF EDEN

Dedicated to my father, John Ivan Unković

Barbara Unković

WEEDS IN THE GARDEN OF EDEN

AUSTIN MACAULEY
PUBLISHERS LTD.

A CIP catalogue record for this title is available from the British Library.

ISBN 978 1 84963 547 9

www.austinmacauley.com

Published (2013)
Austin Macauley Publishers Ltd.
25 Canada Square
Canary Wharf
London
E14 5LB

Printed and bound in Great Britain

Acknowledgments

With special thanks to my daughter, Rebecca Fletcher; my brother, Colin, and his wife, Sarah-Jane; my husband, Denis; and my good friends Rino Gavranić, Petar Franić and John Dean. Without their help, support and friendship this book would not have been possible.

Contents

Recipe Index

Introduction

It's eight o'clock in the morning when the elderly German couple dismount from their ancient, rusty pushbikes and lean them against the concrete sea wall before they wander towards the clear blue Adriatic Sea.

The husband is the first to remove his faded, blue, dressing gown, exposing his flabby belly, which has no hope of ever being covered by his sagging g-string. His wife with her waist-length, grey hair is a little better dressed in her grubby, white, towelling, bath robe and when she takes it off, fortunately, her purple bathing suit is one piece, even if it doesn't quite hide her lumpy fat, with its high-cut legs.

The locals, who live nearby, look upon this scene with horror as it unfolds. 'How dare these foreigners parade themselves on our beach looking like that,' they think. Of course, it doesn't occur to them that they often look just as horrific when they go to the beach. Shedding their multitudes of dark, winter layers, the local women suddenly sport bikinis that are far too small and only just cover their bare essentials; girls, who really are no longer girls, wear bikini bottoms without tops and men prance and strut about in Speedos that should have long since been consigned to the rubbish.

Perhaps that explains the looks we're getting from the locals now that they've found out that we intend to be permanent residents in this village. Surely they don't think we'll be polluting their village and their eyes like these German people, or do they? We've heard that many people here hold the view that, having fought for 800 years to gain independence, Croatia is at long last only for Croatians, and foreigners are not welcome.

However, for me it shouldn't be a problem as my family have been living in this village for the last seven generations.

1
The Beginning

August 2000

My father's blue eyes had become huge now. Oval saucers monopolising his thin, ashen face.

"Let's go for a drive," he said to me. "I won't be able to go out at all soon." His voice was sad and I didn't quite know what to say in reply, especially as what he said was true, but I did *not* like hearing it.

He had always liked Sunday drives. It's something I remember particularly about my childhood. His favourite route nowadays, since he had moved to town, was driving west out of Kamo heading towards Dargaville. It was rolling, green, dairy country and having been a farmer for most of his life he still enjoyed looking at rural pastures and animals.

We pulled up beside a stream, swollen to overflowing by a winter rainstorm. Debris was being carried downstream at a fast pace. The larger pieces were snagged on a dead tree, which had lost its hold on the bank of the stream and fallen in.

Neither of us spoke for a time. Me, because I was at a loss for words and felt like crying. As to what he was thinking, I didn't want to go there.

"I've always wondered what Croatia would be like. I'll never find out now. It's too late. I should have plucked up the courage to go years ago. Now, I'm not just old, I'm sick. But you know, I never did like flying. I only ever left the country once. That was that trip to Fiji. It was enough for me." His voice was quiet as he stared out of the windscreen. The raindrops had turned themselves on again and the windscreen, which was already blurry from my tears, became even more obscured.

Two months later, my father passed away.

The conversation we had while parked beside the stream keeps coming back to me. *I* am going to Croatia.

2
Dubrovnik

September 2005

Our plane bursts out of the cloud and there below us are the magnificent red roofs of Dubrovnik. On the coast, vast limestone ridges rise almost directly from the brilliant, blue sea, which is flat calm. Yachts and a small green island complete my idyllic view. I'm overwhelmed. It is so much more picturesque than I imagined. The colours are so clear and bright.

With reluctance, I drag myself away from the beautiful vista as we are almost ready to land. Now, my immediate concern is Customs and Immigration. We have not been given any entry cards for this new paradise and this could be a problem.

Regardless of our possible impending predicament I can't stop smiling. My excitement is overflowing. A mute, unsmiling official stamps our passports and the customs officer who is reading a newspaper shows absolutely no interest in the incoming passengers. Our entry is quick and easy. Entry cards are not required here and I couldn't be more delighted that there is nothing to spoil my arrival here.

As we leave the airport, my husband foolishly tells our taxi driver that I speak good Croatian. This absurd exaggeration causes a rapid stream of Croatian to pour from the driver's mouth and I can't understand a word. Fortunately, it doesn't matter; he doesn't notice my lack of response as he is too busy proudly pointing out landmarks, including several bullet-ridden houses destroyed during the war in the early nineties. He is friendly and talkative and makes me feel welcome.

The road snakes away from the airport towards the old city. In some parts, it has been carved out of the rocky hillside. The rugged, barren countryside is very distinct. Craggy, grey, stony hills, so close to the sea, mesmerise me, even though they look thoroughly inhospitable. Dotting the landscape are old, stone houses, all with red tile roofs; Cypress trees grown tall and misshapen with age; countless olive trees and grape vines. Looking down on the old walled city from the winding road is breath-taking. The sea is the bluest of blues. The walls surrounding the city are huge, cream, caramel stones and not grey as I had envisaged. They are so immense. I can't imagine the time and effort that would have been required to build them. Apparently they are amongst some of the most complete fortifications in the world.

We have come to a stop. It seems we can't go any further as cars aren't allowed in the old city. Our taxi driver hails a woman walking past and asks her where to find our street. He's heard of it but doesn't know exactly where it is. What sounds like a heated conversation develops between them. Their voices are overly loud to the point where they are shouting at each other as they wave their hands in the air. During the next few days I realise that this colourful way of being is typically Croatian and normal. Several times, the woman shouts, "I don't know!" Until, finally, they sort it out. It's basic Croatian and as they are speaking reasonably slowly I am lucky enough to understand most of their conversation.

Our street is fifth on the right off the Stradun, which is the main street. I am confident we will find it, but I can see by his agitation and the look on my husband's face that he is not.

The Pile gate, one of the entrances to the old city, has a drawbridge, like a medieval castle. As we enter the old city our suitcases make a loud clunking noise bumping along the millions of flagstones, which have been worn smooth and shiny over the years. I'm glad it's not raining as they would be treacherous in the wet.

The narrow, cobbled streets have their names carved in stone at the entrance to each one. They all begin at the Stradun above, the wider central main street, and form a giant maze or grid. Our street contains a big, old church surrounded by an army of cats. They are motley, battered, and streetwise, but I'm happy to see that someone loves them; they are clustered around bowls of food, scoffing at a furious pace. Our suitcases are cumbersome and Denis waits by the church while I continue, checking street numbers. We need number seven, but the numbers do not run in sequence. There is definitely no number seven and now *I* am getting frustrated.

Sure enough, there is no number on the big green door, which leads to our apartment. The proprietor, who has just arrived, is somewhat vacant and cold. It seems to be more than just a language barrier. She is definitely odd and doesn't appear capable of smiling. Maybe, she is just having a bad day.

The apartment door is so heavy I can't push it open, therefore we decide it will be better if I wait downstairs while Denis goes up to the second floor, with the owner and the suitcases. Jetlag is beginning to creep over me, and I'm feeling weak and shaky as I prop myself against the stone wall beside the door. The oldness of the stone walls around me is incredible. It's as if I can feel the history. Dubrovnik with its beautiful Renaissance architecture has been called *'The Jewel of the Adriatic'* and it's not difficult to see why. I am already hypnotised.

Denis' face has no trace of a smile as he comes down the stairs and comments that the apartment is homely. I'm not sure I like his choice of words or the flat tone of his voice. No doubt I'll just have to see for myself. As he heaves the green door open, the smell of cat pee is acute and it follows us up to the second floor.

Almost as soon as I'm inside I start laughing. There is nothing too terrible here, just a small, tacky apartment with worn-out chairs, ill-fitting curtains, threadbare sheets and towels. It is all rather hideous, but we will manage to survive here for the next three days. Apparently, breakfast is supposed to be part of our package; however, the owner has omitted to mention it and there is nothing here to suggest a meal of any sort, unless of course you count the open packet of stale muesli.

We are exhausted on our first night in Dubrovnik and enjoy an inexpensive, simple, pasta dinner early at the restaurant downstairs. Later, in our lumpy, sagging bed, even the raucous noise erupting from the bars and restaurants below is not a problem and we are dead to the world within a short time.

Early the next morning we begin to explore the old city. The rest of the tourists appear to be still asleep. Our noses have led us to the local bakery. They have good croissants, grain breads and other local pastries such as burek, a filo-type pastry of Bosnian origin, which is filled with cheese or meat. Coffee will have to be later as we cannot find any cafés open at seven thirty in the morning.

Shortly after eight o'clock, we are first in line at the booth to buy tickets to walk the walls around the city. We intend to beat the heat and the tourists. At the top of the first major flight of steps, the views in all directions are spectacular and they continue for the hour and a half it takes us to complete the walk. There are plenty of steps, especially up to the towers, and my legs are quivering before we have even gone very far at all. As we look out over the city there are many new, red roofs visible on the buildings below us inside the city walls.

From November 1991 until May 1992, Dubrovnik was bombed daily by the Yugoslav Federal Army from its position on the high ground to the east of the city. At least 2000 shells fell on the city and 70% of the buildings were damaged. Most of the restoration has now been completed with the aid of international funds and today, there are only a few ruined buildings, which I imagine are beyond repair, remaining. Scars from bullets and shrapnel are still clearly visible on many structures.

For me, 1991, when Croatia became a republic, seems some time ago yet the aftermath of this civil war is still clearly visible here in the centre of Dubrovnik. When Croatia's President, Franjo Tuđman declared Croatia's independence perhaps he thought things would progress as smoothly as they had in Slovenia when independence was declared there only a few weeks earlier. However, this was not to be. Croatia's request for republican status had already been turned down twice by the commission attached to the Hague Conference on Yugoslavia. Croatia had failed on two counts. The commission considered that Zagreb, the capital, was not in control of all of its territory and secondly Croatia had not provided adequate guarantees for the protection of its minority population. Tuđman was near-sighted and his declaration of independence immediately triggered a series of uneasy skirmishes between Serbs and Croatians throughout inland areas of Croatia.

Tuđman demanded written pledges of allegiance, for the defence of the homeland, from government workers and civil servants. Many Croatians who were not prepared to do this fled Croatia for overseas at the first available opportunity, many with nothing other than a suitcase full of possessions. Large numbers went to nearby Slovenia and others went further afield to countries such as New Zealand and Australia. In 1991, approximately 200,000 people left the country.

Things came to a head in October 1991 when the Serbian President, Slobodan Milošević, ordered the Yugoslav People's Army (JNA) to attack the interior town of Vukovar. Tanks and artillery levelled the town. This abhorrent atrocity became the catalyst for the beginning of civil war in Croatia.

As the war progressed, the hills from Dubrovnik all the way north to the Pelješac Peninsula were occupied by the JNA and also by the Montenegrin reservists who supported them. Croatian inhabitants were driven out from inland areas close to Serbia and also Knin, inland from Split. During this time the JNA Navy shelled Dubrovnik, Zadar, Split and other smaller, coastal towns.

Gradually, over a period of about two years, the Croatian Army (HV) began to drive the JNA back across the border into Montenegro thus freeing southern Croatia where Dubrovnik and the airport are both situated. During the liberation of the seaside town of Cavtat, south of Dubrovnik, the Croatian Army came upon one of Tito's summer houses. The house was closed up but undamaged. An extensive wine cellar and a stock of expensive cigars provided magnificent extravagances for a victorious celebration party courtesy of Tito. The soldiers showed their respect for Tito, who was a hero for many of them, and once the party was over, left his house as intact as they had found it.

Having secured the coastal towns from the north to the south, the Croatian Army moved on to protect the half a million Croatians who were living in Bosnia Herzegovina. Initially, they began fighting against the JNA with the help of Bosnian Muslim troops, however, when the JNA retreated, the Croatian Defence Force suddenly found themselves in combat against Bosnian Muslim soldiers. This confrontation ended with the very unfortunate destruction of the famous bridge in Mostar.

By early 1995, though the United Nations had created safe zones in many areas of Croatia and Bosnia Herzegovina, Croatia was not satisfied and decided to launch Operation Storm under the command of Ante Gotovina. Using heavy artillery, Croats wiped out Serb Reservists and Militia (Chetniks) from the area around Knin. It was one of the bloodiest slaughters of people in the inland villages of Croatia during the war. Somewhere in the vicinity of 150,000 Serbs fled the country. Bill Clinton, the new President of the USA gave Operation Storm his full support, suggesting that perhaps this would provide a solution to the Yugoslav conflict. The international community at large were shocked by Clinton's support of the 'ethnic cleansing' of Knin and its environs. Ironically, Tuđman actually denied that Croatia was engaged in cleansing the area of Serbs.

The Croatian Army achieved victory and on August 5 1995, the Croatian flag was hoisted in Knin. This date is known as Veteran and Homeland Victory Day and is now a public holiday throughout Croatia.

Today, five Croatian Army officers, including Ante Gotovina, have gone on trial before the International Court of Justice (ICTY) in The Hague, charged with war crimes.

About half way through our walk, on the wall close to the sea, we unknowingly stumble upon an argument between an elderly man and his wife. She shouts at him mercilessly as he cowers silently on an old, white, plastic chair. It reminds me of when I was a child in New Zealand, when my Croatian grandmother used to shout in a similar fashion at her son, Bill. She accused him of being useless, lazy, and good for nothing and told him to go and get a job! This was a regular occurrence and he usually just shrugged his shoulders and wandered off.

Near the arguing couple, we discover olive and lemon trees smothered in fruit. Growing in the vegetable gardens beside two ancient churches they are an unexpected, pretty, green sight, right in the middle of the city.

More of my childhood memories surface as we come upon hydrangeas and geraniums growing in pots outside the door of an apartment. My grandmother always grew pots of brightly coloured geraniums and hydrangeas formed the hedge around the boundary of her property. I remember playing hide and seek underneath the hydrangeas with their massive pink and blue heads. I've often wondered how she managed to have both colours in the same place. In my experience they are usually the same colour. Was it the soil or perhaps the fertiliser she fed them?

As we continue our walk on the wall near the sea, we have a splendid view of a restaurant outside the wall set up on the undulating rocks. It's a magnificent spot with an entrance through an archway at the bottom of the wall. White linen table cloths and silver cutlery gleam and shine in the sun. We make a mental note to go there one night.

From the wall we have spotted a little café, just outside the old town on the side of the hill. Its name *'Pinky'* appeals to us and we trudge our way up the hill in search of coffee. It's good and definitely welcome after our trek around the wall.

As soon as my legs have recovered, we wander through the streets of the old town trying to decide which museums and galleries we should visit. There are quite a few and before we have gone very far, I become side-tracked by a souvenir shop. Usually I avoid such places; however, his one has stone pots and crucifixes carved out of pale stone from the islands of Brač and Korčula. The crucifixes look very similar in style to the ones my grandfather and great grandfather carved out of kauri gum in New Zealand.

After lunch, as we have not been able to shake off our jet lag, we decide to have another sleep. The afternoon is hot and sultry without a breath of wind; the holey curtains on the window of our bedroom remain motionless.

We walk to the small boat harbour near the Ploče gate, past the old ladies knitting and making lace as they sit behind their stalls in the hope of enticing tourists to buy their hand-crafted wares. After a refreshing swim in the sea we feel almost normal again. Rocky outcrops are prevalent here and stainless steel ladders provide access to the sea, which is very clear, and surprisingly warm. It's a lovely spot sitting on sun-warmed rocks in the late afternoon.

In the evening, at the end of a peaceful afternoon relaxing in the sun, we choose another simple, inexpensive pasta meal, followed by a visit to a small museum honouring the fallen defenders of the Croatian National Guard during the occupation of Dubrovnik from 1991 to 1993. Approximately two hundred men were killed in the defence of the city and the museum has an emotional atmosphere. Their photos adorn the walls and we are shocked to see that many of them were young, barely past their teenage years. A large number of them were shot by snipers as they patrolled the city walls. During this time Dubrovnik was completely surrounded by the JNA and totally cut off from the outside world and the inhabitants were without water, power, telephones and an adequate sewerage system for almost two years. The population inside the old city had doubled as residents from the nearby villages fled into the city for safety inside the walls. As I look at the photos of these brave heroes, I feel humbled and tearful.

Before breakfast, we head out of the Pile gate for an early morning walk. Our path takes us through a small park and then onto a narrow path, which leads to the sea. Not far from the water's edge is a monastery. This ancient stone building, on a large parcel of land, looks as if it's been here for centuries. Monks' brown habits are draped over an old clothesline and there is a large, well-weeded vegetable and herb garden. It is calm and quiet here, but I'm disappointed. I was hoping to see a monk or two. Pine needles crunch under our feet and the smell is pungent as we make our way back to a breakfast of cherry strudel.

Our next stop is an extremely, old chemist or apothecary in the Franciscan Monastery. Stone vessels and jars with labels for ancient remedies on them are, but a few of the artefacts on display. The pharmacy has been in continuous operation since 1317 and is still operating today.

On display, inside the old pharmacy is an unexploded artillery shell from the Civil War. The astounding holes in both the roof and the half a metre thick wall, where the shell entered the building are both very visible. I don't think I will ever forget the half metre long shell. It's simply too scary and massive. I count myself very fortunate not to have been living here during the war.

Also inside the Monastery is a small art gallery. High on the ceiling of the gallery are frescoes, most of which are still in good viewable condition. Unfortunately, loud-mouthed, unruly tourists drive us from these two places. Although there is a sign requesting silence and banning the taking of photos, the tourists here pay no attention to either.

A large, over-fed German tourist with a very fat stomach has strayed into the courtyard in the middle of the Monastery.

In this peaceful oasis, where citrus trees and medicinal herb plants are flourishing, he wanders around pointing and shouting. What a hideous spectacle he is in his rumpled, green safari suit and tractor-tyre sandals. His grating, loud guttural comments completely destroy the ambience of this special place.

It is all too much, especially when the ticket seller tries to draw the tourists' attention to the signs and they ignore him. Disgusted by the careless tourists we leave and emerge into the bright sunlight in the Stradun, glad to have left them behind.

Standing next to Big Onofrio's fountain at the end of the Stradun, is a tall, gracious minstrel dressed in a 17th century velvet costume. He captures my attention completely with his lovely, singing voice. I imagine he is a local, but his clothing makes me think he could be either Italian or Croatian. In fact, he appears to have come straight from the pages of *Romeo and Juliet.* He's cute and I can't take my eyes off him. My dalliance, however, is not impressing my husband who is showing distinct signs of annoyance, especially when I decide to buy one of the minstrel's mementos. Still lingering, I choose a small, gold heart from the basket on his arm. He speaks with a thick Croatian accent as he asks if I would like my photo taken with him and of course I would! It is with reluctance that I pull myself away. There is something about him. It is more than his romantic appearance. He radiates a lovely aura.

A visit to another gallery. This one has 'before' and 'after' photos of the Civil War. There are tragic photos of buildings on fire; pleasure boats that have been shelled and are sinking in the harbour; distressed old people sitting exhausted and bloody with their heads in their hands; dead bodies and funeral processions with hand-wheeled carts and the saddest, most worn out mourners I have ever seen. The photos of the Stradun bear no resemblance to the Stradun as it is today. It is absolutely deserted and its beautiful stonework is bullet-scarred and the timber windows and doors have been destroyed and obliterated. The damage to the city was undeniably devastating. The display is well done, but very graphic, I find it distressing and I'm not willing to linger.

It's cloudless and sunny and, as it's not too hot, it's a great day for a picnic lunch. After a visit to the bakery and the general store, for picnic provisions, we pick up our swimming togs and head for the swimming spot we discovered the previous day. All the picnic items are local – bread, cheese, fruit, chocolate and red wine. Our picnic is so good that by the time we have finished eating, the only thing left is some bread. While feeding the pigeons with the left-over bread, I notice a peculiar pigeon that has something wrong with its neck. Quite a distance from us and not easy to see, it is standing on a rock overhang by itself. As it turns around the mystery becomes clear. A complete ring of baguette is around its neck, like a bagel. It looks *very* funny. '*Breadneck*' tries to join the other pigeons, but they are terrified and drive it away. It flies to a remote spot high up on the wall where it perches alone. I think the only way it will remove the bread will be to get it wet so it disintegrates or if the pigeon turns its head upside down, and it falls off, which seems quite unlikely. I wonder what will happen to it.

Today, we say goodbye to Dubrovnik. It is a beautiful, old city and I know we will return.

3
Zadar

The road is busy and the traffic is crawling as we begin the drive up the Adriatic coast towards Zadar, where I have cousins. I am curious and excited to be meeting them soon.

My grandmother Jela, or Nellie as she became in New Zealand, was born in Gradac, in Makarska. She was sent to New Zealand in about 1920, for a prearranged marriage. She and my grandfather Matteo produced seven children, my father being the oldest. In 1945, when he was only 56 years of age,

Matteo contracted a kidney disease from which he did not recover. At twenty years of age, my father became head of the family. He was expected to run the farm, look after his mother, his grandmother and his six siblings, plus other members of the extended family who lived in a second farm house. Shortly after his marriage to my mother, my father inherited the farm when my grandmother moved to live in Whangarei. I grew up living on the farm until I moved to the city at the end of my schooling.

My grandmother never returned to her homeland but kept up a long correspondence with her niece, Ruza, who she never actually met. Ruza now lives in Zadar with her son and daughter and their families. Before we left on this trip, I rang Ruza's telephone number and had the following conversation with her son, Dejan. Ruza was out at the time and as she speaks no English and I spoke virtually no Croatian at that time, it was probably just as well Dejan answered the telephone.

"Alo!" Says a gruff male voice.

"Hello! This is your cousin Barbara Unković calling from New Zealand." There is silence on the other end.

"Hello, hello!" I repeat but still he doesn't speak.

"I am Nellie Unković's granddaughter," I say, hoping this will get a reply and after a few more seconds it does.

"I know *you*! I am Dejan. You are cousin. Yes?"

"Yes. I am your cousin. I am coming to Zadar in September and I would like to come and meet you and your family."

There is silence again and I assume I am speaking too quickly for him so I repeat my last sentence slowly.

"What!" He shouts.

"I will be staying in Arbanassi and I will telephone you."

"What!' His voice is blunt, but I find it humorous as he shouts at me again, and it's then I realise that whoever taught him English did not teach him that he should say 'pardon me,' when he doesn't understand, and that it is rude to say '*What*'.

After I repeat my last sentence *much* more slowly, he responds with,

"Ok. That's good. How old are you? Are you married?"

I am completely surprised by his question and I think perhaps he sees me as a prospective wife!

He ignores my reply and shouts,

"What!" Once more, followed by,

"I am forty-eight and I am *not* married!" The call is becoming too much for me and I must end it before I start laughing hysterically. I say goodbye and promise to call when we get to Zadar.

The drivers here seem almost insane as they pass in places where there is absolutely no vision. Most of them are driving big powerful cars, like Audis. It is no wonder the road toll in Croatia is so high. I find it scary as these speedsters come around the bend heading towards us on the wrong side of the road. It is difficult enough getting used to driving on the right, without worrying about someone crashing into you. Plus, I feel as if the car is about to hit our stone walls or vegetation on the right of the road.

As we pass through the tiny corridor of land that is Bosnia Herzegovina, the terrain remains the same, but the buildings are distinctly different. Their construction looks shoddy and they have a real Communistic, temporary, ugly appearance. We are not allowed to stop and do not wish to!

Our next stop will be Trogir, a town with a Heritage listing about half an hour's drive north of Split. An acquaintance in Dubrovnik suggested we stay in Trogir as she believes it is smaller and more personal than Split. Certainly, the outskirts of Split do not look inviting. Rundown houses and industrial areas litter the landscape, reinforcing our decision not to stop there. Rain is threatening as we approach Trogir. We share a small pizza for lunch in a restaurant next to the harbour and a large, blue umbrella shelters us from the big, fat drops of rain, which have begun to fall on the flagstones around us. The pizza is good, especially the large, green olives on top. I think I am addicted to them. Although they look like Spanish olives, their taste is far superior.

Trogir is contained within a watery boundary by impregnable, impressive walls. There are boats of all shapes and sizes in the harbour here – a sailor's paradise. Luckily, the rain eases up enough for us to look at the beautiful, old buildings and churches that make this town so special. Our accommodation for the night is in a small, renovated hotel, in the centre of town. It has no view but is very clean and tidy.

We are on the road early the next morning. It has rained heavily during the night and there are numerous slips and large puddles of water making the old, tar seal road even more treacherous. The islands off the northern coast of Croatia have come into view. There are three hundred of them and the sight is endless – clusters of red roofs bright and wet with rain. The traffic is just as slow as yesterday with road signs that are either non-existent or unclear. We can't find our way out of Šibenik and my husband's temper is fraying.

"For God's sake! Can't you read the signs? This road is going nowhere. It's a dead end. Now, thanks to *you*, we're lost!" He shouts at me. I ignore him, which seems to make him even grumpier! Then, without warning, he suddenly slams his foot too heavily on the accelerator while he is turning left and the car takes a giant bunny hop across the road, gravel shooting out from the back wheels. I can't contain myself and my unstoppable laughter causes tears to pour from my eyes. When I glance across at him as I wipe my eyes with the back of my hand I see that, thank goodness, he is laughing also.

The road rage is over in time for us to get our first scenic glimpses of Zadar. As I consult the small map and instructions to get to our accommodation in Arbanassi, a suburb of Zadar, I realise that Denis has not spoken for some minutes and the atmosphere in the car is tense again.

"Go left at the next intersection," I tell him. But what does he do? He goes right. He has a thing about turning left, it seems.

"What are you doing? I said *left*!" I shout unable to help myself.

"You did *not*!" He responds, shouting also.

"Anyway, you can't turn left there." He tries to make excuses for having turned in the wrong direction.

"You mean *you* cannot turn left there, more like it," I say.

His response is to ignore me. He knows *I* know he refused to turn left so I ignore him. We are now hopelessly lost in a series of narrow lanes. I can't find any of the street names on my map and still he continues to drive on. I know that each turn he makes, takes us further and further away from where we want to go. He is in an ugly mood now and I really don't know what to say to him so I remain silent.

Ahead of us now is a large parking area; he turns in and pulls to a stop. After several silent moments, I conclude that I will call Vanja. We will be staying at her house in Arbanassi and I know she speaks English well. When I explain our predicament to her, and the fact that I can't find any of the relevant street names, she suggests I give my mobile phone to one of the locals so that she can work out where we are. I approach a group of people waiting in a bus stop and in pidgin Croatian, I try to persuade one of them to talk to Vanja, but none of them will take my phone. Most of them are elderly and actually seem terrified of it!

Denis is wandering around muttering to himself and when he stomps off across the road I assume he is trying to find out where we are.

"Look it's a hospital," he shouts from over the road. "You should know that's where we are."

"Hospital, why should I know that? It doesn't say so in English and I don't know the Croatian word for 'hospital.' Besides, there are no doctors and nurses so why should I think it's a hospital?" He must be able to see something I can't.

"Maybe it's a nuthouse," I suggest sarcastically. To my relief this remark snaps him out of his mood and when I tell Vanja that we are in a car park by a hospital she knows immediately where we are and says she will drive over and we can follow her back to her house. The way to Karma Street takes us through a series of narrow one-way lanes and without Vanja, it would have been very difficult to find.

The apartment is old but spacious and spotless. There are quaint things here, such as the snow white, lace-edged pillow cases and sheets. Croatian woman are renowned for their beautiful lacework and there are some fine examples of it here.

From the balcony, we have a wonderful view of the offshore islands. Once again, the sea is a brilliant blue, even brighter than the sky, which is now cloudless.

Our apartment is at the beginning of a promenade around the edge of the sea. An afternoon stroll takes us to a small café/bar with a terrace at the water's edge. The coffee is satisfactory, but the fat German tourists, in micro bikinis, are an unpleasant blot on the landscape. Later on, during the afternoon, I telephone my cousin Dejan who seems to have been waiting for my call all day! It's a brief conversation and he says he'll call me back when he has spoken to his sister about us getting together.

"What is your number?" He shouts.

"Zero"

"What!" He shouts again.

"Nula," I say.

"Ah yes. You have more in Croatian?" He asks.

"Devet, tri, pet," I reply.

"You are good, very good," he chuckles, not realising there isn't much more to my Croatian yet than what he has just heard. I wonder what he will be like. The only thing I know about him is his age and that he isn't married, nothing else.

At five o'clock, Dejan, his mother, Ruza, and his sister, arrive in a humorous small green car that reminds me of a frog. During the introductions they are polite but rather cautious and standoffish. I'm not sure what to think. In the earlier conversation with Dejan, when I suggested coming to their house he became very defensive and insisted that they would come to us. He was adamant.

Ruza is a carbon copy of my grandmother. At seventy-seven, she does not look her age. Her body is stocky but not particularly fat. She is well-dressed in her navy and white, spotted skirt and blouse and gold, flat-heeled court shoes. Her immaculate, silver hair has a hint of mauve in the front and I can see she has got 'dressed up' for this occasion. Dejan is in casual, long shorts and sandals. He is an absolute cartoon character with his blockhead, cauliflower ears and missing teeth! His sister, Katarina, looks pretty in her floating, floral dress and high heel sandals.

They have arranged for us to meet their good friend who is an English-speaking 'turistic' guide who will take us on a private, walking tour of the old city of Zadar.

The tourist guide is waiting for us in a bar where we all enjoy a drink together before setting out. Ruza insists on sitting next to me and once seated she begins to take family photos from her bag. The first photo she shows me proudly is a very old one of my grandmother holding her daughter Mary's hand. Mary is aged four. Then the tricky part comes. I must tell them that my grandmother died in 1984. They must have known she had died; otherwise, she would be ridiculously old by now, as she was born in 1899. However, the point was that her letters to Ruza just stopped and no one else in the family wrote to say that she had died.

While talking about family, with Dejan and his sister translating for their mother, we learn that Ruza's husband was killed in the war in 1991.

Our walk around the city takes a good couple of hours. The old town of Zadar, which is surrounded by some remarkably intact walls, is accessed by four gates; the streets are laid out in a grid and offer a mixture of architecture from Roman to Baroque. There are twelve old churches and some Roman ruins among the many magnificent sites we are shown, complete with running commentary. Ruza's phone rings often as we walk and I am surprised to see a seventy-seven-year-old with a mobile! Dejan looks comically bored during our walk and insists on stopping often for a cigarette or a beer. His sister and the guide tell him off persistently for his inattention. He really is humorous without even meaning to be.

The highlight of our walk is the sea organ. Newly created four months ago underneath the steps on the promenade by the sea, it is the world's first pipe organ that is played by the sea. There are thirty-five musically tuned tubes with whistle openings on the sidewalk. The movement of the sea pushes air through the pipes and depending on the size and velocity of the wave, musical chords are played. It's incredibly beautiful water music and I love it.

We've had a lovely afternoon with my cousins and their friend and thoroughly enjoyed their company, yet they are still rather reserved and it takes quite some insistence from me to persuade them to join us for dinner. But, in the end, they agree and suggest we go to one of their favourite, traditional, Croatian restaurants. It's another interesting walk through a maze of paved, narrow streets to our table at the rear of the restaurant in a secluded courtyard. The four of them take charge of the menu and order. The local delicacies they choose include individually battered small fish, mussels, which look like our new Zealand cockles, calamari, local bread and black (we call it red) wine. It is a fabulous feast, which we finish off with Croatian maraschino liquor.

We have all had plenty to drink by the time the topic of families comes up again. Ruza's maiden name is Šeric. The 's' is pronounced as 'sh' and the 'e' as 'a'. For some reason Denis has failed to grasp this. Maybe he isn't paying attention or perhaps he's had too much wine and he totally mispronounces the word, not once but several times. All the faces around the table except ours become very serious as they exchange glances. I can see something is not quite right. I am trying to work out what the problem is when Dejan suddenly cracks and begins laughing with gusto.

"Denis! Do you know what you are saying? The word you are using means to have a shit! Now say after me 'Sharrich', not 'Serich'. Have you got it?

"Serich," repeats Denis. Oh my God! He's still got it wrong. It must be the wine! Surely he's not drunk. He's a very moderate drinker and seldom drinks too much, but he doesn't seem to be able to grasp this Croatian word at all. Ruza suddenly catches my eye and then she too begins to laugh followed in quick succession by everyone. In between his batches of mirth, Dejan is still attempting to get Denis' pronunciation correct. Sometimes Denis manages it. Sometimes he doesn't. It's almost like a form of dyslexia. By now, everybody is screaming with laughter and my cousins' inhibitions drop away.

Katarina, who is now very relaxed, takes on the task of explaining their caution towards us. Last year, when they had their first ever visitors from New Zealand, they had a bad experience. These particular visitors insisted that they were family and came to stay, basically uninvited. They were dirty and smelly, didn't wash, and slept on the floor, not in the beds offered to them. It was a very unpleasant experience and to make it worse my cousins just could not fit them into the family tree. Concerned that we might be more weirdoes from New Zealand, they decided they would treat us with caution; however, after today and this evening they have now decided we are genuine and they trust us. Listening to their story, I don't know who the people from New Zealand were either. I guess we will never know. It has been a special evening and Katarina invites us to lunch at her house the following day. She did have plans to plant olive trees, but she will postpone this as she would like us to meet the rest of her family.

As we part company at the end of the evening, Dejan calls out,

"What's that word again, Denis?" It's a humorous end to a colourful, Croatian evening.

The following day we thread our way back through the narrow streets to a street called Put Murvice for the family lunch. We are shocked by their apartment building. It's really hideous – a large, grey, concrete monstrosity with peeling paint. I imagine it is another hangover from the communist era.

Inviting food smells are drifting out from the stairwell as we enter – a welcome distraction from the appearance of the building. My cousins all live here in different apartments. It's not their ideal choice of home and they hope to move to something better when money permits. After losing their original home and all their possessions, they have had to start again from scratch. It is hard for me to imagine being in this situation and it makes me realise how fortunate we are to live in New Zealand. Zadar took quite a pounding during the war and Ruza and her grandchildren were sent to a family property on an island after their home was destroyed. Ruza's husband was home on his own when their house took a direct hit from an artillery shell. He was killed instantly and all of the families' possessions were lost. As is the case during wartime they received no insurance or compensation. The remaining family members continued to work at the insistence of the government; otherwise they would lose their jobs. Shells were falling around them and they too were without electricity and water. It all sounds like such a terrifying experience.

As we enter the fourth floor apartment, the family are waiting for us. With solemn expressions on their faces, they are standing behind their appointed places at the table, which has been elaborately set. The table cloth is beautiful, handmade, Croatian lacework. It is very touching and I have a lump in my throat. Ruza's granddaughters are here with their husbands. Both women are pregnant, which is a source of delight to them all as, since the war, they have developed passionate feelings about the continuation of their race.

Because of the terrible time they endured during the war, I have great admiration for this family and the way they have picked up the shattered pieces of their lives and moved on. Their incredible strength and determination is an inspiration. One granddaughter has since become an economist and the other a judge. Their younger brother Drazan, who is more than two metres tall, is hoping to become a member of the national basketball squad. They tell us he is a very, talented player.

During the shelling of Zadar, Drazan was so terrified and traumatised that he developed an uncontrollable, shaking lower jaw. It was, in fact, so extreme that he was unable to eat or talk properly. I am so pleased to see that he has now recovered fully and exhibits no noticeable after effects. Time and courage have enabled him to move on and pursue a professional sports career.

Lunch is completely homemade. Noodle soup, gnocchi and salad followed by kolac and sladoled (cake and ice cream). They are such wonderful, friendly, hospitable people, and our plates are constantly refilled. It all tastes so good that I cannot refuse second and third helpings washed down with several glasses of superb, local, red wine.

I have mixed feelings when it is time to say goodbye – pleasure at having met all these lovely people and sadness to be leaving so soon. Later, I discover that I have left my sun hat in their apartment. Somehow, I'm unable to go back to get it as I feel that if I do, I will start crying. Thoughtfully, Dejan returns it later in the evening while we are out walking.

It's another early start tomorrow to drive south to Drvenik to catch the car ferry to the island of Korčula, the birthplace of my grandfather and his family.

4
Korčula

We drive the inland route south, through the mountains this time, having already driven up the coast with its magnificent, sea views. Our journey takes us through unwelcoming, mountainous terrain stippled on the flatter areas with fruit covered, wild olive and fig trees. The numerous, small villages we encounter are almost ghostly with their noticeable absence of people. The buildings in the abandoned villages are nothing more than derelict, bullet-ridden shells. This area was a stronghold of Serbian Militia and the Croatian farmers, who were either driven out or killed, have not returned. There's no doubt that this is a terrible consequence of the war and as such the Croatian Government is now offering subsidies in an attempt to encourage families to return to places such as these.

Out of the mountains now, we wind down a steep breath-taking road, heading towards the sea adjacent to the Makarska region or the Croatian Riviera as it's known. The road has been chiselled out of the mountainside and has tight, hairy corners, not to mention the steep grades. I find it frightening; however, the view is nevertheless dramatic.

The ferry to Korčula doesn't leave until five thirty this evening enabling us to spend the day on the beach at Drvenik, a tiny, seaside town nestled in front of the Biokovo Range, which provides a magnificent, rugged backdrop for the sleepy, little village. The air temperature is more than thirty degrees and we swim off and on all day in the crystal, clear water. Unsightly, fat, German tourists, once again in their micro bikinis, plague this beach also, but fortunately we manage to find a spot at the far end of the beach, well away from them.

The ferry crossing to Korčula takes two and a half hours and it's a fine, calm evening allowing us to look at the panoramas all around us. As we sail past the island of Hvar, the smell of lavender is pungent, which seems amazing considering that we are not actually very close to the island. Our progress seems slow as we motor around the tip of the largest peninsula in Croatia, which is called Pelješac. It cuts north-west from the mainland and is one of the major, Croatian, wine-growing regions. Up close it is stony and barren.

Our arrival in Korčula is on time, but unfortunately it's dark and there is no moon to light the way. We are heading for Račišće, a small, fishing village ten kilometres from Korčula town where my grandfather was born, but left when he was a small, baby. The road along the edge of the sea is narrow and winding and in the dark, progress is difficult and slow. Several times, I think we are going to drive off the road into the sea, but twenty minutes later, we round the last corner and look down into a small bay lit with old-fashioned, brass lamps. Račišće is a beautiful, moonlit sight. We can just make out the outlines of the old, stone houses; however, we're unable to find any street signs. Actually, there are no streets, but we don't discover this until later. We are looking for Altea Travel, our accommodation agent as we drive slowly along the deserted foreshore.

As I am the only one who speaks any Croatian, I am elected to ask for directions. There is a lit doorway with an open door not far away and as I walk towards it, I try to start thinking in Croatian and steel myself for the 'no speak English', which I am sure I will get in a village as small as this. I knock on the door and a middle-aged man looks up from cooking on the stove.

"Dali govorite Engleski?" I enquire.

"Pretty well actually, mate! I'm from Perth." He has a typical Australian accent, it is so funny. I am so surprised. This is certainly not the reply I was anticipating, but, what a relief.

"Are you Australian?" I ask him.

"No, I was born here, but I have lived in Perth for a long time. I'm here for a month doing up my mother's house." His name is Ante and he knows the whereabouts of the travel company and points us to the office above the post office.

We will be staying with Natasha and Igor Botica and after helping Denis bring in our bags, our hosts invite us for a drink. It's our first taste of rakija, the local firewater, and it's powerful! Definitely not for the faint-hearted. After two, small glasses, I'm unsteady on my feet! It's time for bed in this quaint, little, attic apartment on the waterfront, which looks like a house for hobbits with its sloping roof and limited head room. My sleep is undisturbed; nothing wakes me, not even the hourly ringing of the church bells next door.

While eating breakfast on our balcony the following morning, we watch the locals as they go about their day-to-day existence. Neighbours gossip to each other outside their homes; women are returning from the shop, post office or the fish vendor; a couple of men are cleaning fish on the small, stone wharf at the end of the bay. A slow pace and a great deal of talking seem to be prerequisites to live here. This becomes even more evident as we go for a walk to explore the cobbled walkways and check out the local store.

Most of the houses here were originally built three hundred years ago and several of them are now uninhabited or in ruins and sadly the population is declining. In 1953 it was as high as 1,400, but now it is less than 400.

From 1900 to 1945, the village derived its income from trading ships owned by local families. They traded timber, olive oil, stone and wine. At the end of World War Two, Josip Tito, who became president of Yugoslavia in 1943, nationalised the fishing industry and forcefully removed the village fleet of thirty-five ships, paying the owners little or no compensation. The ships were put into service trading for the State of Yugoslavia. One village family, who did not want their ship to be seized by the communists, courageously sank their ship. Some years later, when they decided the time was right, they refloated it and sold it privately for a good price.

Migration from Račišće began around 1900 when both jobs and money first started to become scarce in the village and in the years that followed, as the village remained unchanged, migration continued.

At the end of World War Two, at the time the ships were taken, there was large-scale migration when large numbers of people went to New Zealand, Australia and the USA in search of better opportunities and worthwhile education for their children.

Today, the seafaring heritage continues as many of the men in the village become seamen; with several of them attaining elite ranks as captains or masters.

Opportunities for employment here in other fields are limited and today's young people must leave the island when they reach approximately fifteen years of age, to attend professional schools in the larger cities. Once they are qualified, most of them do not return.

The substantial terraced hillsides, which ascend steeply behind the houses, remain in remarkably good condition and are a sight like no other. Thousands and thousands of stones have been stacked carefully and efficiently to make walls. Donkeys transported the stones and it is beyond my imagination how long it must have taken to build so many miles of walls. The majority of the terraces are now disused, whereas they once grew grapes and olives. I've never seen anything quite like them before and I find it difficult to stop looking at them.

There are about fifty small boats anchored in the bay. Most are old and wooden and several are badly in need of repair. Men sit in groups talking, playing cards, or boules. The atmosphere is timeless and relaxed. As we wander the small paths we don't encounter many tourists, but that's not surprising as it's now past the height of the tourist season. The village has one general store or small supermarket, a primary school and a post office. If you need anything else you must go to Korčula town.

Our first lunch on the terrace of our hobbit house overlooking the sea is all local fare purchased at the village shop. It's very, well priced and fantastic – cheeses, dates, bread, olives, and tomatoes, all washed down with a local merlot. We have yet to drink a bad wine in Croatia. No matter what they cost, they have all been very drinkable. The only item, which we both think has room for improvement, is the bread. It's dry and tastes more like cardboard. Having eaten and drunk far too much of this brilliant, quality food and wine for lunch we are left with no other option but to retire and sleep it off.

It's a hot sultry afternoon and we are back on our terrace after a siesta. A little, local, fishing boat has tied up below us at the small jetty. A weathered, old woman in a blue, floral housecoat waits patiently with her bowl and her cat for a handful of small, shiny, silver fish.

We've spent the afternoon reading and lazing in the sun; however, it's now time to cook dinner. We're having pasta and it really won't be as tasty as it should be without olive oil, which strangely enough the shop doesn't sell. There is only sunflower oil, which won't suffice. When we ask the shop owner, he agrees to sell us a bottle of oil from his own trees. When his wife returns with it, ten minutes later, it's in an old, plastic bottle, which once contained iced tea! It's thick, green, spicy and magnificent, the best I have ever tasted. Later, we learn that some of the local oil producers here have won prizes in Italy for their extra virgin olive oil.

Our hosts have suggested we visit Vaja, a beach about a kilometre out of town. Stocked up with a decadent picnic, which of course includes wine, we drive most of the way, which seems lazy, but the picnic basket is heavily laden. At the end of the asphalt, we pick our way down a steep precarious track over large, broken rocks, along the cliff edge, down to the pebble beach. Until 1951, Vaja was the site of a stone quarry. The pale-coloured marble, which is softer than marble but harder than limestone, was primarily used for house building. Layers of multi-coloured stone are still clearly visible on the side of what must have once been an impressive quarry.

A beautiful, little bay awaits us at the end of our walk and there is not a soul in sight. The beach is made up of stone pebbles of all shapes and sizes. Luckily, I have brought my reef shoes. There is only one, small dwelling on the waterfront here and it looks as if it's a holiday house that has recently been renovated. It looks wonderful; however, the long hike up the hill from here and the thought of carrying shopping home negates the little house's magical site.

What a heavenly day in the sun it's been, swimming, reading and, of course, our picnic, which included excellent local Kraš chocolate. Later that day, back in the village, we come across a special book – *A history of Račišće*. The book details the first settlement of Račišće in approximately 1680 by refugees fleeing the Turkish invasion of Herzegovina. The initial inhabitants were a group of about ten families who it is thought were sponsored by the Catholic Church. I am able to trace my family back to one of these families. Although the Croatian text is a challenge, the pictures, old and new are outstanding. There are also several references to my family – Unković. The families in this village all have nicknames to avoid confusion as there are a large number of people with not only the same Christian name but the same surname as well. My family nickname is Mravac, which means ant or small and hardworking! The book spurs me on to search for with living relatives here. To begin with we arrange an appointment on Friday, with the local priest as we would like him to offer a blessing for my deceased family.

The two churches in Račišće are side by side. The new one was built one hundred years ago and the little, old one, which is no longer in use, three hundred years ago. The new one is open today and we go inside to light candles. The stud is very high and the interior old and ornate. As I look around it occurs to me that my grandfather and his family would have sat in this very church as I am today.

In the evening, as we drink a glass or two of red wine on our terrace, enjoying the beautiful sun set with fiery pinks and oranges as the sun sinks below the horizon, I feel I could stay here forever.

We are up earlier today and after a breakfast on our terrace of fresh figs, pomegranates and yoghurt, courtesy of our hosts, it's time for a walk. In the village cemetery, I am eager and excited as I begin to follow the trail of my ancestors. Wandering amongst the headstones, I am disappointed to find that none of the marked graves belong to my family. In the end, I come to the conclusion that they must be buried in either the very, old, unmarked graves or under the flagstones at the entrance to the old church in the village. The only way I can find out is to check the records for burials in the register in Korčula, but I will need to improve my Croatian before I attempt that. For the moment, I must be content to meander through the wild, yellow, crocus flowers around the tiny chapel in this well-tended, pretty, little cemetery.

As we are walking back from the cemetery, the priest drives towards us up the street. I must say that he deserves the prize for being the worst driver in the village. With his feet hard down on the accelerator and the clutch, he hops his way up the street in fits and starts causing the engine of his old, rusty Yugo to rev menacingly. Fearing he will run us down, we take refuge behind the nearest fig tree. What a sight! The grumpy, old bugger with his down-turned mouth grips the steering wheel tightly as he disappears past us up the hill. We can't stop laughing as we emerge from the safety of the tree. We have seen him walking around the village. The locals always speak to him, but he is sour and aloof in return and reminds me of the unfriendly Irish priests of my childhood in

New Zealand. Apparently, his excuse is that he is from Lumbarba, another village on Korčula, and he doesn't want to be in Račišće! Sometime later, we also hear that he used to be attached to a church on Pelješac, but he was kicked out after behaving badly. We're not sure what he actually did and in reality we don't want to know. I wonder what our audience with him will be like?

At this time of year, the villagers begin work early in their vineyards and olive groves. In fact, they are coming home at about seven in the morning, just as we are getting up. The most fascinating sight is the wrinkled, old women, dressed in black, trudging home with enormous piles of sticks strapped to their backs. They are collecting firewood for winter. The men come and go, weed eaters strapped to their car roofs, having cut the grass around their olive trees. There are a huge number of these particular machines here, which indicates just how many thousands of olive trees there are, in and around this village. Now, in September, the olive trees are heavily laden with drupes and the grapes too, are big and fat. Wooden wine barrels have begun appearing on the waterfront ready to be filled with seawater to swell the timber and close the cracks. Harvest time must be near. As the days tick by I continue to be fascinated with the day-to-day life of the people of Račišće.

Today's the day we will talk to the priest. I have my request written in Croatian, ready as we knock on his door. It's open and we can see inside – a spacious, old, stone building with high ceilings, wood panelling, and ornate, expensive looking, antique furniture.

"Molim!" He calls out sourly. He is sitting behind his desk as we enter and he does not ask us to sit down, although there are several chairs in the room. We stand uncomfortably in front of him and feel the chilly atmosphere.

"Dobar dan," I say to him and hand him my note with as much of a smile as I can muster given his sourness. He reads it and his eyes become glazed. He mutters a few words in Croatian with a very peculiar accent. No doubt it is because he is not from this village. He and I exchange a few words. However, I can tell by the look on his face that I am not making any progress. He stares at me coldly and begins to talk over the top of me.

"In Italiano!" He shouts.

"Non!" Says Denis. "Français!"

"Oui Français," He agrees.

Denis' French is reasonably fluent, he having lived for a time in Paris. However, the priest's French is terrible, almost unintelligible. We are having difficulty understanding him when suddenly we realise that he is not interested in listening to our request at all and that the only request he will entertain must come from our hosts in writing. Having imparted this little gem he then decides he's had enough. It's time for us to leave and all of a sudden he shouts,

"Do videnja!" Giving us no choice but to go.

We have been invited to have lunch with our hosts and their son, Mario. It couldn't be better timing as I will be able to talk to them about the priest's request. We eat outdoors on their terrace under the shade of a massive creeping vine that covers the roof of the terrace. The menu consists of cheese, pršut (local smoked ham), bread, salad, grilled eggplant, sausage and lamb. The lambs here drink salt water and the meat has a distinctly stronger flavour than New Zealand lamb. Igor proudly produces red wine from Pelješac; this is our first taste of wine from this region of Croatia and we are very impressed.

We are anticipating language difficulties during lunch as Natasha speaks only a little English and Igor doesn't speak any at all! However, we get by with a lot of laughing and joking. Igor is curious to hear about my family and when I show him the papers I have, including my grandparent's marriage certificate, it turns out that Igor's grandfather who lived in Waiotira, near Whangarei, was one of the witnesses at their wedding. Finally, near the end of lunch, I pluck up the courage to tell them about our visit this morning to the priest. Natasha telephones him and he tells her that his calendar is booked up a year ahead for blessings and if we want it done then the cost will be fifty kuna per person. What an unreasonable old fool he is!

At two minutes to six, we sit, waiting in the church. We have decided to attend tonight's service regardless of the priest's attitude. Apart from the two of us there is only one other woman here for this evening's service. A couple of seconds later, the priest enters through a back door and when he sees us he turns bright red, becomes flustered, and rushes back out the door. Well, perhaps he does actually have a conscience after all. There are no more takers for his service by the time he reappears with a piece of paper in his hand.

Half an hour later I have lost interest in his dull monotone voice and I am considering leaving when his voice suddenly changes tone and to my astonishment, he includes my family in his prayers. I wonder who or what caused that. Perhaps it was just his conscience!

Today's destination is Korčula town. We'd like to explore the town and also do some shopping. As we head back along the road bordering the sea, the wind is funnelling through the channel between Korčula and the Pelješac Peninsula. Today, it's easy to understand why it's such a popular destination for wind surfers. As we round the last corner where a pretty lavender garden covers the grass verge, Korčula town with its spire and bright, red roofs sits majestically before us.

The town was named by the Greeks after the black forest (Korkyra Malaina) that can be found covering the spine of the island. Set on a tiny knoll, Korčula is still completely surrounded by thick 13th century walls. The main streets rise up to a small, central square where the old entrance to the town is a majestic, fortified tower called the Revelin. Viewed from a distance, the age old town has a quaint medieval appearance. The busy marina adjacent to Korčula is overflowing with crafts of all shapes, sizes, and ages. We admire a line of seven, elegant, old-fashioned, cruising yachts rafted together. Approximately twenty metres long, in another life they were trading ships before their conversion to tourist vessels.

Parking in Korčula town is free and not too difficult. The actual town is smaller than we imagined, but if you look closely everything is there, from banks to butcher's shops.

There is a small market in the centre of town where we can't resist buying local cheese and dried figs before we walk around the perimeter of the town adjacent to the sea wall. Here, we are underneath a canopy of ancient pines, which creak and groan with age as the wind rustles gently through them. Many of Korčula town's restaurants are here, lined up in a row along the sea wall, menus displayed prominently. I think it would be difficult to decide which one to eat at with so many to choose from. Opposite the sea wall the houses have ornate carved decoration, intricate balconies, and windows dating back to the 15th and 16th centuries.

Across the other side of town there is a small supermarket with a bigger, better range of bread than our village store, including pumpkin bread. The selection of vegetables here is also plentiful and fresh. We are unable to resist buying fat, red paprikas (capsicums). The banks here have long hours, eight till eight every day except Sundays. The one we choose is not busy when we go in to withdraw money. In the centre of town there's an unusual outdoor movie theatre where they also hold performances of The Moreska, a traditional sword dance, which came to Korčula from Italy in the 16th century. Its popularity is thought to be linked to the struggles against the Ottoman Empire. It is performed in Korčula every Thursday evening during the summer season and has been for four hundred years. There are a good number of clothes shops here also and from my first, quick, look the prices seem reasonable if not cheap. Most of the garments are locally made in Zagreb or imported from Italy. I will come back on my own, when I have more time. Shopping for clothes is not Denis' thing!

We are on our way back to the car, when a funny, toothless, old man materialises in front of us and begins calling with a soft, clucking sound. He carries a parcel wrapped in white paper and a bottle of water. At the sound of his voice, cats begin to appear and follow him. He reminds me of the Pied Piper as he limps along with a rolling gait and sparse grey hair sticking out in all directions. First, there's a marmalade cat, then a black and white spotted one, a multi-coloured kitten followed by a large, grey tom with a well-muscled body and huge, rabbit-like feet. Several more cats slowly emerge from the nearby bushes. Underneath an olive tree in the tiny park, the old man sets out plastic dishes. One by one, he puts food from his parcel into each bowl, chatting away to the cats in Croatian as he goes. The only one to keep his distance is the grey tom who is considerably bigger than the rest. I wonder if he is the leader. It is a very touching sight as I lean over the wall to watch.

Today, we are going to explore the western end of the island as we head towards the port of Vela Luka. As we leave our village, the road is steep and narrow for the first five kilometres. There are several hairpin bends with few places to pass another vehicle. Fortunately, we don't encounter any other traffic and I am relieved when we reach the village of Pupnat at the top of the hill. Pupnat is in the middle of nowhere; it's smaller than Račišće and has a rather dilapidated appearance. The only thing of notable interest in this village is the road or track as it is really, which was built by Napoleon in about 1806. As the island of Korčula was considered by Napoleon to be a strategic position in France's war against Prussia, Napoleon built a military road along the spine of the island. Almost all of this road has long since been rebuilt and it forms the main route from one end of the island to the other. The only stretch of the original road that remains is this piece in the village of Pupnat.

From the highest elevation in Pupnat the sea is visible on both sides. The Pelješac Peninsula can be seen to the north and the islands of the southern Adriatic to the south. Pupnat is the highest point at this end of the island, but unfortunately though the views are fairly stunning I don't find this village with its dejected air and rural outlook, at all inviting.

We drive on through the inland villages of Čara, Smokvića, Blato, and finally Vela Luka. The scenic drive through the spine of the island takes about an hour. Korčula is heavily treed in most parts and the landscape is lush and green. Along this route, there are of course the inevitable olive trees and grape vines. Both the green and black grapes are almost ripe and I can't help noticing the absence of birds. I find this surprising considering there are no scarecrows or netting protecting the vines.

An interesting archaeological museum claims our attention in Vela Luka. Its main attraction is the collection of archaeological finds from the nearby prehistoric cave at Vela Spila. There are various artefacts including pottery; animal and human remains; stone axes and flint knives. The earliest records of settlements on Korčula date back to the Neolithic Age, six to eight thousand years ago. The remains of two adults, which are on display in the museum, were discovered in 1986 and scientific research has dated them back to the Neolithic period.

Later, after coffee and a wander along the waterfront, we drive back in the direction from which we came but by a slightly different route, which takes us through Brna, a small sleepy village with hardly a soul in sight. The houses in Brna are much newer than in Račišće and Vela Luka and lack character. Close to the beach we pass a small dated-looking hotel called Hotel Feral. The name has us both laughing. It seems most unfortunate. We learn later that feral means lantern in Croatian. Brna has a small, deserted beach where we spend a quiet afternoon swimming and lying in the sun.

On the road again, we stop at the Pošip winery and museum in Smokvića for a tasting and to admire the old wine-making equipment. We buy half a dozen bottles of wine, the first of which we will drink tonight with a pizza from one of the two cafés in our village. Exhausted after our outing we indulge in a siesta and have only just gone to sleep when we are awakened by singing. The neighbours have had a long lunch or perhaps a celebration and the men are singing with strong, melodious voices. Obviously, they are not shy when it comes to singing in public. It's lovely to listen to and we thoroughly enjoy it even if it did wake us!

The singing comes to an end and is replaced with loud voices. The family next door are stacking firewood in readiness for winter. The smell of wood sap is strong and I enjoy inhaling it as it drifts in our windows. A handsome (in spite of his big nose) suntanned, strong-looking man of about thirty-five is unloading the wood from the back of a station wagon.

"Dobar dan!" He calls out with a friendly smile. His eyes are bright blue, as bright as my father's. I begin conversing with him in my limited Croatian but soon find I don't need to as he speaks English very well. Ranko was born in Blato, which he tells me means mud, in English. He is married to a girl from Račišće and now lives here. He is very passionate about his country and my first impression of him is favourable. I like him. At dinner, our Pošip red wine is full-bodied and a good choice to drink with our big, four-cheese and olive pizza. We can't fault the pizza. The local cheeses and olives are superb and it's the equivalent of $7NZD. During dinner, we meet Gorga, a painter who specialises in restoring frescoes in old churches. She is holidaying here, as she has done for many years. Her home is in Zagreb where she was born. She's friendly and refreshingly different and we enjoy her company. Gorga's hair is striking – absolutely white, not grey or blonde, but white. I cannot tell if it's her natural colour or whether it has actually been dyed and it is impossible for me to ask her as I've only just met her. I find it most intriguing, as are her bohemian-style clothes. Apparently, she has lived and worked in Paris as an artist and also in China where she was a costume designer for the opera Aida when it was performed there in November 2000. At first glance it is immediately obvious that Gorga is definitely not a local woman. She has far too much flair.

As we stroll back to our apartment after dinner, we notice everyone who lives near the church sweeping and tidying in front of their houses. We assume it's in preparation for tomorrow's wedding. The 'hen' party took place a couple of nights ago, beginning with the noisy evening exit from the village of a red car packed full of giggling girls. Their departure was accompanied by much horn blowing and it was obvious who they were. We couldn't help hearing them return at five in the morning either, as more horn tooting was combined with drum beating and singing! If it wasn't such a novelty for us I'm sure we would have been irritated to have been woken up so early.

It's a fine day for the wedding and two hours before the ceremony is due to begin, most of the guests are gathered outside the bride's house drinking, and by the time they walk to the church, a number of them are very unsteady on their feet. One of the most inebriated is the flag bearer at the head of the procession. It's a merry meander, complete with a vocalist and an accordion player. The church service is protracted and it is some time before the wedding party and their guests emerge and return to the bride's house for more drinks prior to attending the reception at a restaurant in Korčula town. Their departure from the village is accompanied by more car horns and this time the din from about thirty horns is deafening.

The customs surrounding weddings in this village are very unusual. Once a commitment is made between the couple they may live together before they are married. But, they may only marry with the approval of their families once they are financially stable and once the woman has proved she is fertile and produced a child, preferably a boy. What happens if the woman fails to become pregnant? Well, it has happened to at least one couple here. The man's family put pressure on him to end the relationship and when he finally bowed to his family's wishes, rumour has it that he became an alcoholic, his would-be bride left the village and she is now on medication for depression. This custom is apparently peculiar to this village. Other villages on this island have different customs, such as in Blato where it is common to have a mistress with the knowledge of your wife. It is so blatant that all three of them can be seen having a drink together in the local bar.

The quantity of alcohol consumed by the people attending the wedding was obviously large and we wondered about them being picked up for drink driving as the allowable blood alcohol limit at the time of writing is 0%. Apparently, the police turn a blind eye to wedding revellers and it is understood that if there are any car accidents the guests will all contribute towards the cost of any repairs.

Today, the weather is cooler and the sky is filled with heavy, dark clouds. The mistral is blowing from the south and though our bay is sheltered, the sea is covered with white caps. Unsurprisingly, as we look out to sea an assortment of yachts are making the most of the breeze. As it's not a good day for the beach we have decided to drive to Korčula town to visit the local archive in the town hall.

The man in charge of records is busy on the telephone and we must wait. His office, which is in an old building, has shelves full of dusty books, which make me feel like sneezing even though I haven't touched them. On the windowsill, drying in the sun on a newspaper is a small, wet, brown teddy bear. I wonder whom he belongs to and why he is there? Finally, the man we are waiting to see hangs up, but to our dismay, he tells us that the records here start at 1894. This is no help to me as the information I am looking for will be contained in the earlier book, therefore, if I want to continue my search I must go to Dubrovnik.

I am disappointed with my visits to the priest and the archive in Korčula and in an attempt to try to forget about them, we go for a brisk walk along the road that runs across the hillside at the back of the village. A storm is brewing and the wind is whistling through the pine trees. Growing wild here, there is an abundance of figs, grapes, blackberries, walnut and almond trees. Oregano and sage flourish too and I crush them under foot as I walk. Their smell is intense; far more potent than their domestic counterparts. It's extremely special to be able to wander and enjoy such natural beauty, so close to the village. As the first drops of rain begin to fall, unfortunately we are forced to abandon our walk and seek the shelter of our apartment.

The following morning, the weather is still unsettled as a squall blows into the bay and we are forced to close the windows and shutters, against torrential rain. Luckily it passes within fifteen minutes, but not before soaking the children waiting for the school bus and a little tabby cat sheltering in vain underneath a cypress tree.

As it's not beach weather again today, Denis suggests a drive to Dubrovnik to the Drzavni Archive.

The archive department is located on the first floor of a beautiful, old palace and the man who specialises in genealogy, Nikola, is very keen to help me. The records are contained in huge, old books with heavily bound covers. The elaborate handwriting is in ink, some Croatian, and some Italian on heavy, grainy paper, which has become yellow with age. To preserve the books, members of the public cannot touch them and Nikola almost tells me off when I accidentally touch a page in my over-excitement at finding a familiar name.

Without any difficulty he finds my grandfather's birth record and the birth and marriage records for four generations earlier. Nikola is very happy to make copies of the documents, which we can collect in a couple of days. I am well pleased with what I have found and we will pick up the copies on our way to the airport, when we leave Croatia at the end of the month. They cost about $5NZD and when we collect them our obliging genealogist has a surprise for me. He has drawn up a family tree from the information contained in the documents. He is such a helpful man.

The tiring trip back from Dubrovnik through heavy traffic leaves us without the energy to cook dinner on our return to the village. Tonight we will eat at 'Konoba Vala' in Račišće for the first time.

The stone building that houses the restaurant was built in 1700 and is close to the water's edge. Vedran, the owner who is also the chef, explains that he has only just taken over the premises and is slowly revamping the place. Vedran is from Rijeka, in the north of Croatia; he is well-travelled and interesting. His English and Italian are fluent and he is very friendly and professional with a hilarious sense of humour. The menu is large and varied and after some initial indecision I choose crayfish risotto and Denis, black (squid ink) risotto. Both are particularly good. Denis, however, struggles with the boiled silverbeet and kupus (a cabbage-like vegetable commonly found in Croatia) but I love them. My grandmother cooked silver beet often when I was a child.

There is no chance of sleeping in today. Something is happening at the church. Normally, the bells ring on the hour and half hour twenty-four hours a day and at church service times, there is extra ringing. This morning, the bell ringing started at eight o'clock and an hour and a half later, it's still going intermittently. As our apartment is almost next door to the church the sound is extremely loud and imposing. Natasha tells us that a trainee is practising. Unfortunately, the trainee does not have the touch and by the time the ringing stops, we have definitely had enough.

Denis is on his way to the shop when he meets Clare. Although Clare was born in New Zealand, she has lived most of her life in Australia where she met and subsequently married Tom. Tom's mother was Australian and his father is a Croatian born in this village but living in Australia. Tom and Clare first came to Račišće about eight years ago and fell in love with the village. They purchased an old house on the waterfront, which they have totally renovated and turned into a very successful bed and breakfast business.

Clare has heard that we are in the village and as she has lived here for a number of years, she thinks she might be able to help me in my quest for family history and the whereabouts of my deceased ancestors. She is close to sixty and would once have been extremely attractive, but too many years in the sun and too many glasses of wine, have aged her and she is now well past her best. Regardless of her weathered appearance and full-on manner, I can see she has a heart of gold and would do anything for you. When she gives us useful information about the workings of the 'Katastar' (land registry office) and the church records, it prompts me to mention the priest.

"Perhaps you could help us with the priest?" He is such a grumpy old bugger. We haven't had much luck with him at all," I say to her.

"What do you want from him?"

"We'd like to have a look at his records and see if there's anything there to help me with my family tree," I say.

"No problem!" She says, laughing. "I have him eating out of the palm of my hand. He'll do anything for me. I keep his grounds tidy and he likes me, if you know what I mean!" She gives me a wink. I shudder to think what she means by that remark, but no doubt we'll find out.

This is the first time we have seen the priest so animated! He is sitting at his desk while our friend from Perth stands next to him. She is actually so close to him that her ample bosom is rubbing against his arm as she talks to him and his face is one large smile! Her command of Croatian seems appalling to me and her accent is terrible. There's not a rolling 'r' to be heard. Regardless, it doesn't seem to matter, as within a short space of time she has been given permission to lift the record books off the shelf. Once again, the records are not old enough. The earlier ones are missing and the priest explains that the communists destroyed them immediately after the Second World War in about 1947. Having drawn a blank here, there is not a lot more I can do to find more information about my ancestors. Probably the only avenue left is to talk to some of the old people in the village.

Having now ascertained the whereabouts of the Katastar, it's time to search the old record books to find out what became of the land my family once owned in the village. It's a difficult task in an office still locked in the old communist ways and, unfortunately, my poor command of Croatian makes it even worse. It tries my patience until eventually my persistence pays off and although I have been up and down the stairs and in out of the same office three times, I finally manage to gain entry to the room where all the old record books are kept. With the help of a young man who speaks English (he has actually been to New Zealand), we wade through the lists of houses and land owners where we find many references to my family and my spirits rise as we find their names on several blocks of land. But, unfortunately, when we get a printout from the computer with the up-to-date information it shows that all of this land was passed on or sold to other people in 1900, which is about the time my great-grandfather, his wife and children left Yugoslavia for New Zealand. I was hoping to find I had inherited even a small plot of land and I'm a little disappointed that I have not, but by the time we leave I have had enough of dusty old books and silverfish.

Back in the village, Ranko, the man with the big blue eyes, is walking up and down the water's edge, staring into the sea, as he seems to do several times a day. Today, he has finally found what he is searching for as he pulls an octopus out of the water.

"Will you eat it for dinner tonight?" I ask him.

"No. It must go into the deep freeze for a few days before I cook it. Otherwise it'll be tough. Some time I must make you my octopus salad," he says, blue eyes shining, as he takes his catch away to gut it.

It's late September and the cooler nights remind us that autumn is here. One by one, the old fishing boats are being dragged from the water and repainted. All the local men pitch in together. A small, shiny red and blue one has just been finished and is now ready to be put back in the sea. In a few days it will be time for us to leave and we'd like to enjoy another pizza before we go. Tonight's one includes small, locally caught, blue fish. They're good and go well with the cheeses, tomato, and herbs. Gorga, the fresco restorer, is also eating here tonight and she is very excited. She thinks she may have found an apartment here that she can afford to buy.

"How many owners does it have?" I ask her, knowing that some properties here have multiple owners, making them impossible to buy.

"Just one! And it has clean paper!" She replies, meaning the title is clean. We wish her luck as she finishes her meal and goes on her way.

Shortly after Gorga's departure we unknowingly stumble upon the village nuisance, a Croatian who has returned here after having lived for several years in America. He is drinking at the bar of the pizza restaurant and we cannot seem to escape him. Irritatingly, he persists in correcting our English, Croatian and anything else he can think of. We thought his drunken state was the cause of his behaviour, but the following day he is just as obnoxious as we witness him having a fierce argument with two of the locals. Apparently, one of them caught him throwing stones at his house during the middle of the night! It's a small village and I imagine they may drive him back to America if his behaviour doesn't improve. His American accent won't endear him to the people here as Americans are not very popular since NATO's intervention in the Civil War and some ill feeling towards them is still evident.

When Croatia announced its intention to seek independence prior to 1991, the USA did not offer them their support as they were quite content for Yugoslavia to remain intact. The USA is one of the major powers in NATO and it is considered that this caused NATO's reluctance to intervene during the Civil War. By the time the United Nations became involved in the war and atrocities still continued, NATO finally decided it was time to get take action. Many Croatians believe that the USA, which was by now under the Presidency of George Bush, could have done more to stop Milošević being elected as the leader of Serbia. Neither could they see that the proposed Vance–Owen (VOPP) Peace Plan, which was formulated in part by the USA, actually had many benefits for Croatia. It is considered that in fact Serbia had more to lose than Croatia if the peace plans were implemented, yet many Croatians remained obstinate and failed to grasp this. It would seem that perhaps some Croatian people were possibly too greedy and wanted more territories than the plan was offering them.

Near the end of the war, the USA, with Clinton as their president, supported Croatia in its decision to launch Operation Storm, yet for some inexplicable reason not even this could rid Croatians of their negative feelings towards the USA.

With just two more days left on this idyllic island we have hired a boat to explore some of Korčula's bays, which are inaccessible by road. The sky is clear and blue and there is no wind, as we set off in a little, old, wooden boat and chug slowly past Vaja and Samograd. Our destination is Babina, but by the time we are almost there, the wind has risen and the sea has become choppy. The beach at Babina, which is visible from our boat, is covered with litter (a common problem on the beaches here) so we head back to Samograd to go ashore for our picnic. As this is what is called an FKK (nudist) beach, Denis strips off with the intention of having a swim. Just as he reaches the sea and turns towards me to ask if I'm coming swimming too, out from behind a rock a camera appears! Its owner is naked, old, and skinny. He tries to photograph Denis, but luckily Denis spots him and shouts at him to get lost and the old man vanishes instantly.

We are strolling along the waterfront, when we receive an invitation from a friendly man in the village, also with the surname Unković, to come and watch as he makes wine in his konoba (wine cellar). Antun has recently returned to Račišće after an absence of thirty-eight years. He was eighteen when he left and even though he established a profitable business in New Zealand and built a big house, he could never overcome his feelings of homesickness. Now, he says he is much happier having sold up his assets in New Zealand and returned to the fold of his family.

The wine making is a family affair. Antun and his brother tread the grapes with their feet, in a huge wooden barrel. His sister and aunt are sorting extra, plastic bags full of grapes in the depths of the konoba and from time to time offering advice on the crushing process. The crushers' faces are covered with beads of sweat and their feet make loud, squelching noises. It looks like hard work. The two of them look like twins in their identical, striped blue and white t-shirts and pose proudly for me to take their photo. Antun tells us that this year they had to buy extra grapes as there was too much rain and the grape harvest was poor. He makes wine every year as he believes it's important for them to keep the old traditions alive; he goes on to explain that it's one of the things he missed while living in New Zealand. Apparently most families here still continue to make their own wine and almost every house has a wine cellar. Sure enough, as we walk around the village on one of our last evening strolls, we see large, plastic bags full of grapes and people hard at work in their konobas. The air is heavy with the smell of fermenting grapes.

It's grey and overcast on our last day in the village, and we've decided to have lunch in Korčula town; we can only hope that the weather will hold. We've chosen a restaurant beside the sea wall under the canopy of big, old pine trees and we begin our last lunch here with a glass of dry, white wine from Lumbarda, a village close to Korčula. I am a fan of dry wine and this one is definitely to my liking. The wine is accompanied by excellent brown bread and an aubergine spread. The main course arrives smartly and consists of black risotto with mushrooms; battered, lightly fried, little fish, tomato and potato salad and red wine. It's a big meal, but there is nothing left on our plates by the time we finish eating. It was superb.

In the afternoon back in Račišće, as it's not raining yet we amble along to the end of the wharf which extends out into the bay, to admire the village yet again and take more photos. Ranko comes to say goodbye and brings us a bottle of his homemade, red wine. It's so good we polish off the entire bottle before dinner.

Wind and rain are rattling the shutters as I wake up early on the morning of our departure. I pull the covers over my head and snuggle in feeling very safe and secure in this house made for hobbits. The strong wind has no effect at all on the solid, stone building. My only concern is, will the weather clear when it's time to pack the car, otherwise we will get very wet indeed.

It's been a fabulous holiday, one of our best. I know my father would have loved it here. I think about him a lot as we pack. Igor and Natasha wave us off as we drive out of Račišće. When the village disappears from sight, my eyes are full of tears and my throat is too tight to speak. I am searching for a tissue in my bag, when Denis suddenly tells me to look at the road in front of us. Standing in the middle of it are two pheasants. Birds always remind me of my father. They were always somewhere in his life. He had a thing about them. He called sparrows, spaggers and he used to make a show of shooing them away when they came too close, but he was never serious about it. He could always spot the lovely, shiny, iridescent feathers of a tui before anyone else. And then there were pheasants, the most significant birds in his life.

When I was a child, my brothers and I used to go 'pheasant shooting' with him in his Chevrolet car. Our job was to spot the pheasants. He kept his shotgun loaded, cracked open and ready beside him on the front seat.

"There's one!" One of us would shout as the front seat passenger frantically wound down their window.

"Duck! He'd whisper loudly as he aimed his double-barrelled shotgun out the window.

He was a good shot and seldom missed.

"Can I have the cartridge?" We'd all shout at once. There were different coloured cartridges and we loved collecting them. The same applied to the pheasants' tail feathers. We fought constantly over those. We ate so many pheasants during my childhood that they no longer interest me as a culinary delicacy.

One day, my father did a complete turn around and announced that he would no longer shoot pheasants and he put 'no shooting' signs up all over his farm. Any hunters who tried to trespass onto his land to shoot them were sent away with stern words. I don't know what caused this abrupt turnaround, but I assume it was just the first rumblings of conservation having an effect on him.

On the day of his funeral, as his coffin was being lowered into the grave, I heard a noisy rustling of wings and I looked up in time to see tuis flying out of the nearby trees and then directly over our heads.

For me, the sight of the pheasants on the road was like a message from my father.

5
The House

March 2006

It's been five months since we returned from Croatia to our home in Noosa, Queensland, and I'm still finding it difficult to focus on work. It's very difficult to stop thinking about the unspoilt beauty of Korčula now that I'm back in Noosa amongst brash Australians. Having lived for three years in Noosa, sadly I have come to the conclusion it's not the paradise that everyone believes it to be. Although it's a great place for a holiday, once you live there you realise it's full of old, boring, retired people, refugees who can't function properly in the city, or anywhere else for that matter, self-confessed, know-all gurus, unemployed drop kicks who spend all day surfing and solo parents who are attracted by the cheap rents. All in all, they are an odd assortment inhabiting one of Australia's more beautiful beach areas which, unfortunately, has a very high crime rate. Houses and business are robbed on a regular basis.

My mornings are usually spent in my office at home, working on my computer, before I head in to Costa Noosa Espresso, the roastery and café Denis and I set up in 2003. This morning I will be late as I have received an email that is proving to be a huge distraction. Last week, I began looking at real estate sites in Croatia on the net and ended up sending out a number of emails. There are plenty of properties for sale in Korčula town, but until today I hadn't been able to find any for sale in Račišće. By the end of the day, I can't keep quiet any longer. It's time to confess to Denis what I have been up to and the photo of an old house for sale in Račišće, which I show him, leaves him temporarily speechless. It's a while before he responds and when he does, it's not at all the reaction I have been expecting.

"Oh no! You don't think you are going to do what the olive farm woman did, do you? I knew you shouldn't have read that book! You're not Carol Drinkwater! You're a foreigner. You can't buy property in Croatia!" He says, looking at me as if I've gone mad.

He'd told me that our holiday there had been the best one he thought he'd ever had, so I assumed he would like the idea of buying a house there, but obviously I was wrong.

A couple of days go by and I'm sure we've both been thinking about the house for sale in Račišće, especially when Denis asks me what's wrong with a holiday house somewhere in New Zealand. Unbeknown to Denis, I've sent the real estate agent in Dubrovnik an email asking how foreigners go about buying property in Croatia.

Karl, the real estate agent, has replied explaining that it is best for foreigners to set up a company to purchase property in Croatia; otherwise they must wait for approval from the government. This is usually a lengthy progress and can take up to two years. The email seems a bit dodgy as it goes on about him and his partner, Alan, setting up the company on our behalf and us sending them money! It ends by saying that he'll call us in two hours to see what we want to do. Denis is furious when I read him the email and immediately decides it's a scam.

"Talk about presumptuous. Does he expect us to buy the house sight unseen?" He asks angrily. I have to say, I'm not exactly comfortable with the email either. It's too pushy and presumptuous. However, underneath all Denis' anger I'm sure I can detect a certain amount of interest in the house now, but I don't think he wants me to know that, given his initial explosive reaction.

As promised, Karl rings. Following our conversations with both Karl, who is German and his partner Alan, who is Irish, we both agree that they come across as slimy and non-trustworthy. Before he hangs up, Denis tells Alan clearly that we do not want them setting up a company for us and as Alan is obviously reluctant to let go of us, he suggests we talk to his friend who is a lawyer in Dubrovnik!

"What a pushy pain in the neck. Who does he think he is?" Denis declares as he slams down the phone.

We are both uncomfortable with what we have just been through, and it prompts me to suggest that we just forget the whole idea as it's simply too difficult.

There's yet another email from Karl! He is persistent, I'll give him that. Why don't we just pop over for the weekend and have look at the property? I can't believe it. He doesn't seem to have any idea how far away from Croatia we live. But, that's not the end of it; he has arranged for the lawyer to ring us. Karl and Alan are now really over-stepping the line and I respond by sending them a blunt email telling them we are unhappy with their pushy attitude.

The lawyer from Dubrovnik, Boris, is pleasant and professional. He's spent some years in the UK working as a shipping lawyer and he speaks English well. Without pressing me or wasting my time, he explains that he would be happy to set up a company for me if I want to buy a house. Apparently, he doesn't know Karl or Alan very well, but suspects that they are greasing around him as they want an introduction to one of his clients who is a property developer. He tells me that the real estate industry in Croatia is not regulated and as a result, agents do not require licences and accordingly, they are often crooked and shouldn't be trusted. He goes on to say, I could use them to show me the property, but if I want to buy it, he will do the rest. When I tell him they have offered to set up a company for me, he laughs heartily and replies,

"You are joking with me, yes!"

I like this lawyer. He gets straight to the point and I feel that I could trust him pending my first meeting with him.

After a further discussion with Denis I am quite surprised when he does a complete turnaround and suggests I fly to Croatia to have a look at the house. If we don't check it out then we could go on wondering forever about what we might have missed out on, he reasons. We can't both go and I'm the logical choice as I have considerably more real estate experience than Denis, having sold residential properties in Wellington, for a number of years.

I'm on my way! I will be in Croatia for a week. I have an appointment at the lawyer's office the day after I arrive and Karl will take me to Korčula to see the house two hours later.

My accommodation, which I booked on the internet, is inside the old city of Dubrovnik and it's another hobbit house in an attic! Tonya, the owner, meets me and I am delighted with the recently, renovated apartment. Simple and clean; it couldn't be better. There's a quaint view over the red rooftops and it has a heating unit, thank goodness, as it's the middle of winter here and about six degrees during the day.

The Stradun is quiet as I enjoy a croissant and coffee for breakfast sitting outside in the watery, winter sun. It's chilly and I am very glad that I have my coat, hat and gloves. I can't help but notice that the contrast between summer and winter here is marked. Many of the trees have lost their leaves and their brown branches appear desolate as they reach towards the sky on the hillsides high above the town. In winter, a large number of shops and restaurants are closed and won't reopen until May. There are a few tourists wandering around, but nothing like the numbers that besiege the town in the summer season.

Boris makes me feel very important and ushers me into his shabby office as soon as I arrive. Short, stocky, and overweight, he is casually dressed in blue corduroy trousers and a jersey. A fat cigar hangs out of the corner of his mouth. Even before I sit down his phones start to ring. Clearly irritated by them, he barks bluntly as he answers the calls. They are a constant interruption. Then, just as we are about to get started we are interrupted further by the appearance of a man with an extremely, short, crew cut, standing in the doorway.

"Karl!" Exclaims Boris gruffly, looking none too pleased. "What are you doing here?"

"I thought I'd sit in on your meeting with Barbara."

"You will only sit in, if my client wants you here!" Boris replies in an angrily controlled voice, glaring at Karl, before turning to me.

"Nice to meet you Karl." My response is cool as I extend my hand. "I'll see you later. Eleven at the Pile gate, you said, didn't you?" His expression is extremely cold. Boris gets up to see him out.

"Just making sure he's gone," he says as he sits down again. He is frowning and his face still looks rather angry.

"I'm afraid I don't like him and he is not going to *make* me like him by turning up here uninvited! I nearly told him where to go," he says taking a couple of nervous drags on his cigar. He actually looks quite comical; this cigar-smoking lawyer with the fiery eyes. Having voiced his thoughts, now, he leans back in his chair and relaxes a little.

"I like you. I could see you weren't going to take any nonsense from Karl," he says puffing on his cigar.

"Let me tell you a funny story, before we get started. You don't know anything about Karl and his business partner, Alan, do you?"

"No, I don't," I reply.

"Well, Dubrovnik is a small town and there aren't too many secrets here. So... Karl and Alan. They met after, what do you say in English, a one night stand! They are, um, gay. But there's more. They are... how you call it. They are hidden. Do you know what I mean? I don't know how you call it in English." It took me more than a few seconds to realise what he was trying to say.

"You mean they are 'closet queens'," I reply, laughing.

"Yes! That's it. Oh I like that expression. It's good. Closet queens. Like wardrobe?" He gives a big bellow of laughter as he leans forward and rests the cigar in his ashtray.

"Right, now let's get down to business. Tell me about this house."

It's eleven-fifteen and there is no sign of Karl. I've just come to the realisation that it's going to be very tight getting to the ferry on time if he doesn't get here soon when an old blue Mercedes pulls up in front of me and the driver gets out.

"Hello", he calls out towards me. "I'm Alan. Captain Alan Frampton. You must be Barbara. Karl couldn't make it I'm afraid." Captain Alan is a rumpled individual aged somewhere in his mid-fifties, wearing an old, quilted, blue windbreaker and cheap, brown trousers. His voice has an English accent. As I look at him, I can't help recalling my conversation with Boris and I find it difficult to keep the smirk off my face.

"We'll have to hurry if we're going to catch the one o'clock boat. I hope the traffic isn't too heavy," he says as we drive off.

"What happened to Karl? I saw him earlier this morning and he didn't mention anything about not being able to take me to Korčula."

Alan then tells me that Karl was convicted of excess blood alcohol while driving in Austria and isn't actually allowed to drive as he has been disqualified for eighteen months! Apparently Karl's not concerned about getting caught as he continues to drive around Dubrovnik. Alan says he needs to, in order to do his job and they don't think the chances of him being caught in and around Dubrovnik are very high!

Alan has to really push his old Mercedes in the heavy traffic and I will be surprised if we get to the ferry on time. His overtaking is scary as he passes in places where he shouldn't and I shut my eyes several times as I'm afraid he will have an accident. Alan's mobile phone rings often while we are travelling and as he is so close to me I can hear the voices on the other end. They are business calls from mostly English people and he is so unbelievably slimy and over the top as he talks to them, promising to take them to tile shops, kitchen shops and all sorts. He makes me feel like throwing up, that is if his driving doesn't cause me to do so first.

As we drive onto the ferry, it begins to pull up its ramp and we are nearly left behind! It's all a bit hair-raising and unsettling and I could have done without it. Our first stop is Korčula town to collect the key to the house and also a woman, one of Alan's colleagues. For some reason, to which I am not privy, she is coming with us. Alan also picks up ten litres of local, extra virgin olive oil for himself. It's almost raining, but not as cold as Dubrovnik when we arrive in Račišće. The village is deserted except for the store owner who is outside stacking boxes next to where we park the car. His stomach has grown somewhat since we were here last year. Probably too much stodgy, winter food and not enough work, I suspect. The store hours are reduced during the winter and he is closed between noon and five o'clock. As we acknowledge each other with a wave he takes all of us in and I know he is wondering why I am here.

With an almost tangible feeling of despair, the house stands proud and tall, even after thirty years of neglect. Immediately in front of the house is a large dead tree, old mould covered timber and junk. It's all particularly unsightly as are the black, mouldy walls. As we fight our way through six foot high weeds on the steps that lead to the kitchen and also the main door of the house, it's very evident that no one has been living here for years.

Alan suggests we look at the kitchen first and once he has unlocked the door he gives it a massive kick! Horrified, I ask him why he's being so brutal and he says,

"It'll be full of rats." All of a sudden I get the impression he's trying to deter me from buying this house. But why?

Thick, grey cobwebs hang from the ceiling in the kitchen and all the surfaces are covered with white, powdery stuff. It looks as if a baker has gone mad and thrown flour everywhere! A closer inspection reveals that the ceiling has fallen in and the powder is actually plaster. The ugly, fifties, glass light, which has become detached from the ceiling, is now balancing precariously on the edge of the table. I try to brush aside the cobwebs to look in the dim pantry, but all I succeed in doing is getting covered with cobwebs. My black coat is a mess. Alan thrusts me aside rudely and pushes in ahead of me.

"You'd better not come in here!" He exclaims in a peculiar voice. "There's blood all over the walls!"

I ignore him as I'm sure he's talking nonsense and go in regardless. There are meat hooks hanging from the ceiling, a row of rusty choppers on the shelf and old, dried, blood stains are splattered on the walls. Obviously this was where they used to cut up meat.

"You'll never fix this!" Alan snorts. "What a mess!"

The kitchen still contains everything from plates and glasses to pots and pans. There's a very dead, rusted, fridge and an oil-burning heater, which has leaked fuel all over the floor. Flaking, cracked, bright orange vinyl is visible in patches on the floor and when I prise up an edge in the doorway, to see what is underneath, it looks like terrazzo tiles, but the light isn't really good enough for me to be certain.

"Seen enough? Alan suddenly asks me out of the blue.

"No, not at all!' I respond, outraged. His tone seems to imply that we should leave now before looking at the rest of the house.

The inside of the main house is in vastly better condition than the kitchen. It has two floors with four bedrooms and a bathroom. According to Alan, the owners walked out about twenty years ago leaving all their possessions behind. Cupboards are overflowing with linen, clothes, shoes and countless pairs of underpants!

I wander from room to room trying to assess the bones of the place. The floors are parquet and although it's old-fashioned, the bathroom looks as if it just needs a thorough cleaning. On the upper level, an exterior door opens on to a south-facing terrace of about thirty metres square. A long, wet, jagged crack runs down the middle of the terrace. This is obviously the cause of the slumped, kitchen ceiling. Like the exterior, the terrace is black, slimy and nasty. A rusty gate at the back of the terrace leads to the back path and a small completely overgrown garden.

Inside, at the top of the landing on the first floor an old, blue, wooden ladder is protruding out of the man hole leading into the attic. I ask Alan to hold the ladder so I can have a look in the ceiling cavity and also at the inside of the roof. He groans and complains, but I am insistent and give him no choice. No daylight is visible when I peer into the attic and I can only see one, small hole in the roof tiles. I'm pleased with what I've found and I'd say the roof is in good condition and doesn't need any repairs. The ladder shudders and wobbles as I come down and I'm almost at the bottom when one rung starts to give way. I'm sure it wouldn't hold Alan's weight and he is somewhat annoyed that he cannot climb it.

"What's up there?" He wants to know.

"Nothing!" I reply, not feeling inclined to share my findings with him.

In the konoba, which is on the lowest level of the house, the cobwebs are even thicker, if that's possible. Again everything is still here, blanketed with dust; wooden wine barrels, glass bottles, funnels, fishing equipment and tools. I snap a quick photo and go outside; it's just too cold in there. After one last look at the exterior of the house I'm ready to leave. As we walk back towards the car, Alan suddenly blurts out.

"Well are you going to buy it? Because if you don't *I* will!" He says, causing me to turn towards him and laugh.

"I'll have to think about it."

"Well, come on. What did you think?"

"I *told* you, I'll have to think about and talk to my lawyer!"

Now, I'm absolutely positive he wants this property for himself. Or maybe he thinks he's using reverse psychology on me in an attempt to make me buy it. His behaviour is so strange and snakelike I feel like Eve being offered forbidden fruit in the Garden of Eden.

Alan gives up on my evasive answers and begins to walk quickly down the path, striding ahead of me. His colleague, who has been totally silent, catches up with him and they begin to discuss the ferry timetable for our return to Dubrovnik. They're walking so fast I'm left behind very quickly and I can no longer hear what they are saying. But, I know that they must be talking about me when Alan looks back at me and suddenly gives me a scornful look. By the time I catch up with them at the car they seem to be arguing about the ferry timetable.

"I'm really hungry." I say, fully aware that I am interrupting them. "Could we get something to eat here, before we go?"

Alan gives me another filthy look before saying,

"No. There's no time. We have to catch the three o'clock ferry." His voice is hostile and the atmosphere has become tense and uncomfortable.

The storeowner, Andrija, has been listening to our conversation and walks over to us.

"Hello, Barbara. I thought it was you! How are you?" He asks in fluent English.

"I'm good. Really good, and you?" I reply.

Alan seems to feel threatened and butts in and shouts rudely at Andrija,

"Who are you? Do you know this woman?" Andrija must have picked up the bad vibes and puts his arm around me and hugs me as he replies,

"Of course! She is my cousin!" He's not, but his remark shuts Alan up instantly.

"Let's go!" Alan is sour as he gets into the driver's seat and silence reigns as we drive back to Korčula to drop his friend off, before driving on to the ferry terminal.

The ferry is overdue and there's no sign of it. We've been waiting in the queue for three quarters of an hour when I break the silence.

"Don't you think we should ask the ticket man what's going on?

"It's that Angelo in there and I'm not talking to *him*! So, don't expect *me* to go!" Alan's voice is sulky. Angelo explains to me in English that the ferry has broken down on the other side at Orebić and they are waiting for a replacement. It's impossible not to notice that Angelo is gay, very gay, and I can't help wondering what has gone on between him and Alan. It's another hour and a half before the replacement ferry arrives and by this time I am absolutely starving, but there is nothing I can do about it. It's winter and the food shops at the ferry terminal are closed. Alan sits next to me in a sulk continuously stuffing his mouth with peppermints and does not think to offer me even one.

Shortly after we finally board the ferry, fuddy-duddy old Alan receives the first of about six mobile calls. They are all from the same English-speaking young man and again Alan doesn't realise that I can hear the caller on the other end quite clearly.

"What time will you be home?" Says the voice.

"Soon," replies Alan. His voice is no longer grumpy and he seems to have recovered from his obvious bad mood.

"See you. Bye." Alan's voice is nervous and he disconnects quickly.

"That was T Com. My broadband's down again." He tells me without *me* asking.

"That's no good!" I reply, trying not to laugh. His phone rings again about five minutes later.

"Where are you? Shall I start cooking the dinner?" Asks the voice.

"I'm on the way back from Korčula. You're coming round to fix it tonight. Yes, that's OK. Bye." He sounds embarrassed as he hangs up.

The next time it rings Alan looks at the screen and cuts off the call.

"Business call! It can wait till tomorrow," he says without conviction.

Unfortunately, the caller won't be put off and rings again almost immediately.

"Yes!" Alan answers in a blunt voice.

"Why did you hang up on me? Don't you want to talk to me? I haven't heard from you all day! I miss you!" The voice is upset and petulant.

"I'll be back around seven-thirty and you can come round to fix the broadband then. Bye!" Alan is in a high state of agitation now. When the phone rings, yet again, after looking at the screen, he turns it off and locks it in the glove compartment! Who needs a closet when you've got a glove compartment to hide in?

If I was hungry before, I am past the point of no return now. I have had nothing to eat since seven this morning, but when I suggest to Alan that we stop and get something in one of the little towns along the way, he says we can't as he has to be back for the man from T Com because he can't do without his broadband any longer and it's already been down for three weeks! I give up. My stomach will have to wait.

It is close to eight o'clock when Alan drops me off at the Pile gate. He wouldn't stop at a restaurant, yet he stopped at a winery on the Pelješac Peninsula and took a long time to buy three dozen bottles of wine for himself after saying he would only be five minutes and that I need not get out. I am so glad to see the back of him by the time I get out of his car that I ignore him when he says,

"I'll ring you tomorrow to see what you are going to do!"

I'm cold and tired as I stumble into the restaurant closest to my apartment. The waiter gives me a complimentary glass of rakija, which goes straight to my head. When my meal arrives I'm so hungry I consume my risotto so fast it's ridiculous, but never mind it's time to call Denis and tell him what I've found.

"The house has good bones, I believe. The original old house must have been built 200 years ago, but it's had several alterations since then. The floorboards have been replaced with concrete and there's parquet over the top of that. It hasn't been lived in for 20 years or more and it's pretty dirty and dusty and full to overflowing with the owner's possessions. I mean everything including his underpants! The main house just needs cleaning and painting and all the shit throwing out. The roof is good and looks as if it's been re-roofed relatively recently. I had a look in the attic and could only see one, small hole. There's a huge, south-facing terrace of about thirty square metres, I'd guess. It's two minutes' walk to the beach and you can see the sea from every window. There's only one bad problem and I need to sleep on it. It's the kitchen and the surface of the terrace. There's a giant crack in the terrace above the kitchen. The kitchen is in a small, separate building. It must have been added on much more recently, I think. Anyway, the crack has let water into the kitchen and it's caused a lot of damage. The whole ceiling has slumped in and it's in a pretty bad state. I need to run it past the lawyer I think. He should know more than me about the construction of stone houses. Apart from that I like it. It's a lot of work, but I don't think you'd mind that, would you? Oh and the grounds are really overgrown, but that's just gardening. No big deal. I don't think. Oh and I almost forgot. There's no power or water either and the wiring looks pretty old and dodgy too. I bet it would need rewiring, just because of the age of it."

"Has it got a wine cellar?" Denis asks me.

"Yes. It's huge and freezing cold! All the old barrels are still there. I've taken a great photo of it. I'll download it and the others I took and email them through to you so you can see what you think. I'm tired and I need sleep now. It's been a long day and I want to email the photos to you before I talk to the lawyer again tomorrow. Oh and the real estate agents are revolting. Hideous! A couple of crooked gays who went into business together after a one night stand! There's more but that'll have to wait till I get back for me to tell you. It's hilarious. You'll crack up!"

Although I'm extremely tired at the end of my hectic day, no matter what I do, sleep eludes me. Stuck in my mind's eye is the facade of the house. It simply won't go away and finally I admit to myself that I've decided we will buy it unless, of course, Boris finds something onerous with the title tomorrow. Finally, I drift off to sleep in the early of hours of the morning; the pull of my ancestors, urging me to return to my homeland, is strong.

Next morning, I'm in the lawyer's office by nine o'clock. We discuss the house and its condition in detail. I've thought about the kitchen/terrace problem overnight and feel sure that if you repair the terrace, seal it, to stop the leak and then gut the kitchen, and replaster it, it would solve the problem. I run this idea past Boris and he thinks it is feasible, but says he can't actually tell me it would work. It'll have to be my call. After a long conversation with Boris, I ring Denis from Boris' office and he says we should go ahead with the purchase provided I'm happy.

Boris orders a copy of the title as we need to make sure that the property only has one owner before we make an offer. He also asks me whether I have signed any contracts with Alan or Karl and of course I have not. I do not trust either of them. They are more than simply weird with their odd reptilian ways.

"If they call you, tell them to ring me. I'll get rid of them!" Says Boris, puffing as usual on a fat cigar.

I must go back to Boris' office after lunch and as it's a beautiful, sunny day, I've bought a tasty ham, cheese and tomato, grilled sandwich, a small bottle of red wine and a pastry for lunch and I intend to walk around to the swimming spot outside the walls that we visited last year. There's not a soul in sight as I settle down for lunch, but I should have guessed this wouldn't last on such a magnificent day and before long I am joined by a group of young Italian men. They're not too intrusive until one of them decides to go for a swim and once he strips off the rest of them follow suit. It's a bit of a shock, six naked Italians laughing and cavorting around without a stitch on! They are bold and try hard to catch my attention. Unfortunately, I don't find any of them attractive; they're too skinny and white! It's just as well I've finished my lunch otherwise I might get indigestion.

Back in Boris' office, he has a copy of the title and explains that we have a problem. Apparently the title is not clear as the house is still owned by two people. Originally, it actually had eleven owners. He shows me the list before he tries in vain to call the vendor's lawyer who is not answering his phone. It is his intention to tell him I wish to buy the house and accordingly he will draw up an unconditional contract once the property has been transferred to one name only.

"How long will that take?" I inquire. "And what if someone else comes along and tries to buy it?" (I was thinking about a certain real estate agent.)

"It'll take a couple of months and no one can buy it legally until the title is clear. The matter must be approved by the court. I will make a gentlemen's agreement with the other lawyer that you will buy it and in the meantime, tomorrow, we will set up your company so that we are all ready to go when the time is right. Now, tomorrow, my partner, Ivan, and I would like to take you to lunch. We have somewhere special we hope you'll like. I'd like to make up for the terrible treatment you received yesterday from Alan and treat you to some of our local, seafood delicacies."

Today, Boris' assistant, Dario, greets me. He is in his mid-twenties and has just qualified as a lawyer. Like Boris, he also speaks excellent English. They are, in fact, both accredited court translators. Dario has prepared the papers for the formation of my company and takes me through the process, from the bank to the notary and the court for registration. Everything goes smoothly and all the people involved in this process are particularly obliging. Dario has a very good relationship with them; he's confident and agreeable and I enjoy his sense of humour. By noon, my company has been formed and it's time for lunch.

"Sorry about my car! His is worse. Can you believe it!" Says Boris, laughing.

No I can't believe it. It's an absolute tip and I have to push old shoes and all kinds of stuff on to the floor to make a space to sit and there's nothing I can do about the dog hairs on my black skirt!

"No problem!" I tell him. What else can I say?

We drive to the port area of Dubrovnik, close to the Boris' office. On our way to the restaurant, we walk through a market with dried figs, daffodils, spring flowers and green winter vegetables for sale. It's all local produce sold by an assortment of colourful, local people.

The restaurant is in an ancient building with a curved stone roof. A bar is downstairs and the eatery is upstairs underneath the exposed inside of the roof. It's a fantastic, old building which Boris explains used to be a donkey barn. Boris has reserved a table for us overlooking the bar downstairs and almost as soon as we are seated, a waitress arrives with a water jug and a basket of bread. I can't help noticing as Ivan looks down the front of her plunging neckline. Clearly she loves it and gives him a big smile. I get the feeling he's a bit of a lady's man.

"Do you mind if we order for you? We're right next to the fish market here and we always eat whatever has been freshly caught in the morning. Is there any fish you don't eat?" Boris asks me between puffs of his cigar. He looks as if he is quite dependent on them. It's just as well he is allowed to smoke in here.

The first course, oysters from Ston, on the Pelješac Peninsula, arrives. Very big and plump, there is a gargantuan amount of them. They are equally as good as New Zealand Bluff oysters and when the big, silver dish is empty, it is replaced by another dish loaded up with clams (they look similar to New Zealand cockles). Red wine flows generously and it isn't long before we're all nicely relaxed.

Boris can't wait to tell Ivan about Alan and Karl being 'closet gays'. This conversation almost causes them to roll around on the floor they are laughing so much. During lunch, Boris' mobile is a constant irritation as it rings almost every five minutes. He says it is all Ivan's fault as he never answers his or even turns it on so all the clients ring Boris. There is good-humoured jesting between them and the phone calls are obviously a bit of a problem sometimes, however, today they don't seem to be. Both Boris and Ivan are interested in my family history and also curious to know why I'm looking to buy a house here. Boris is concerned that as foreigners, it may be difficult for us to gain acceptance into such a small, traditional village.

"They can make life hell for you, you know, if they don't want you there," he says seriously before going on to suggest that I apply for Croatian citizenship as he believes that it would make many things easier for me. He also adds that it would probably come through more quickly if he files the application. He's horrified when I tell him that I have heard instances of people lodging their applications in New Zealand and waiting for five years for them to be granted.

The conversation turns to children and we discover we are all on to our second marriages. An obviously, humorous conversation takes place between the two of them in Croatian and Boris tells me that Ivan will be lucky if he isn't on to his third. Didn't I see the way he was looking at the waitress? We all laugh. I've definitely drunk too many glasses of wine and simply must go to the toilet. By the time I return to the table, the next course has arrived. It's a white fish, called mol (it tastes a bit like hapuka) on a bed of lettuce with a side plate of vegetables. It looks good, but Boris and Ivan do not. They have become extremely serious and their faces are long. I become instantly nervous and don't know what to think. What could have happened in my short absence?

"We've got something to tell you," Boris says and the tone of his voice makes me feel even worse. All their laughing and joking has disappeared. What have they had been talking about while I was in the toilet, I wonder?

"Shall I tell her or will you?" Boris asks Ivan.

"*You,* it should be you." Boris takes a deep breath and regards me seriously.

"We have decided your soul is here. And as you belong here, it's right for you to buy this house." His eyes are wide open and passionate. I am very touched and for a few moments I can't speak.

By the time Boris drops me off at the Pile gate it's after four o'clock. I'm cold on the outside but have a warm glow inside me as I remember Boris' words. Over lunch, I believe I received the final seal of approval for my decision to buy the house.

It's my last day in Dubrovnik, my body is aching all over and I'm hot, but I know it's cold. I'm sure I have some sort of flu bug, which is going to make the flight home a very long one. I received one call from Alan, a couple of days ago and managed to avoid him by saying I was busy and couldn't talk. I'm sitting in the airport shivering and shaking when my mobile rings again. This time it's the other snake, Karl and there are no niceties.

"Well have you made up your mind yet? Are you buying it?" His voice is blunt and rude and makes me respond with the bare minimum of words as I tell him to talk to Boris about the problem with the title.

Even though I'm shivering and shaking as I make my way home through Frankfurt and Singapore I know I'm happy with the old, stone house I've decided to buy. It's got so much more to offer than a bach in Omaha, Whangaparoa or the like.

6
The Contract

April 2006

Two months have gone by since my trip to look at the house and I haven't heard a word from Boris. He has not replied to any of my emails. I'm becoming very concerned and finding it difficult to be patient.

Eager to apply for Croatian citizenship, I have all but one of the documents I need for Boris to file my application. I'm beginning to wonder if there is much point now though, as I've heard nothing from him and maybe it will not be possible for us to buy the house after all.

At last the email I have been waiting for from Boris arrives. It begins with apologies for not having responded earlier. He has been in hospital with a heart problem, which isn't surprising considering he is very overweight and also a heavy smoker. The property is now in one name only and Boris will draw up an unconditional contract. We will buy the house, including everything inside it.

I'm so excited I can't wait for Denis to see it. He, however, is a little more cautious than I and suggests that there may be something onerous in the contract, which will preclude us from buying it. I don't believe it and am not prepared to entertain any such negative thoughts!

7

The Land

2002

I've been living in Wellington, New Zealand, since 1994 and it is now two years since my father died. I am shopping for dinner in Moore Wilson's in Central Wellington, when my mobile rings. My father's lawyer from Whangarei, is calling about the land my father once owned in Hewlett's Road, Mata, just south of Whangarei. In the early nineteen-hundreds, when my great grandparents came to Northland, they originally bought two farms; one in Sloane Road and one in Hewlett's Road. Not long after their arrival in New Zealand, two unfortunate catastrophes occurred. In 1903 Ivan, one of their sons, died and then in 1906, my great grandfather, Nicolo, drowned. These events made it too difficult for the remainder of the family to cope with two farms and the bulk of the Hewlett's Road farm was sold. The land they retained, which was inherited by my father as the eldest son, was a section with a sea view, on the highest point of the farm. I believe that someday they had hoped to build a house there.

During my childhood, I went with my father to the 'section' as he called it, whenever he sprayed the noxious weeds there. He regarded the 'section' as a nuisance and was always irritated when he received letters from the local council about the gorse and requests to control it. In August 2000, when he was bedridden with his illness, he asked me to go through his papers to get them in order. He suggested that several of them were out of date and should be thrown away. When I came upon the title to Hewlett's Road his scornful response was,

"That bloody thing, huh, throw it out. I don't own it any more. I gave it to the council in the early seventies. Glad to be rid of it!" I was shocked by what he told me. Even though I had no idea of its size or its value, giving it away seemed a strange and rash thing to do.

Apparently, the council had contacted him in the early seventies saying that they needed to take part of his section to change the course of the road. He made an agreement with them that they could have the entire section on the condition that they waived the outstanding rates on it. According to him, he did not own it any longer. I put the old land title in the rubbish with some reluctance; but he was adamant. Now, his lawyer was ringing to say that the council had never put the new road through or changed the ownership of the section into their name and therefore my father was still the owner. My father's ownership had come to light as the farm adjacent to the section was being subdivided into sections and the developer needed permission from the section's owner, to put in the services. As my father was now deceased, his lawyer transferred the section into the names of my brother, Colin, and I.

After receiving several opinions on the value of the land, we decided to sell it and as it was coastal land in Northland, it was valuable. Colin wanted to renovate his existing house and I put my share in the bank as at that point in time I had no particular use for it. Somehow, it seemed a very appropriate use for my windfall when I found the house in Račišće and I'm sure my father would have thought so, too.

8
Our House

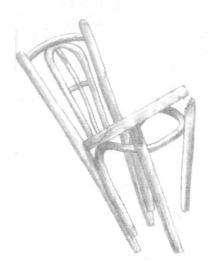

June 2006

This is my third visit to Croatia and the forbidding, grey, stony mountains still continue to hold me spellbound. Our first stop will be the lawyer's office before we drive to Korčula to take possession of our property.

"What do you mean we can't pay the balance today? We told you back in April when we paid the deposit that we would be here today to pay the balance and take possession. We intend to drive to Korčula today. We've come a long way and this is very frustrating to say the least!" I tell Boris in what is most likely an angry voice. Something seems to have gone wrong and I'm having trouble controlling my anger as we sit in Boris' office.

"Yes, I know I know, but the vendor lives in Slovenia and at the moment he is away at sea and he will not be back for six weeks. His lawyer has only just told me. For you to pay the balance, the vendor must come here to receive it personally. It is the only way. It is the law. I will call the other lawyer and see what we can do," Boris replies quite calmly.

It is alright for him, he hasn't come half way across the world to take possession of a house! Boris makes two calls. First, he rings the lawyer and then, the vendor's wife in Slovenia. The result is extremely surprising. He arranges for us to pick up the house keys at a café in Korčula. We can take possession today and pay the balance of the purchase price when we leave Croatia in four weeks time at the end of June.

I have never taken possession of a property until I have paid the entire purchase price! It would be virtually unheard of in New Zealand. But, things aren't quite as simple as I thought they'd be having got over the first major hurdle. We have yet another problem. The vendor's wife insists we can't stay there as the power and water aren't connected. Undeterred, we decide to take our chances and assess the situation when we get there. On the outskirts of the village, Denis stops the car and I stare yet again in awe at the quaint, old village nestled on the doorstep of the brilliant, blue sea. Will there ever come a time when I am no longer drawn to the ancient, stone terraces dotted with olives and cypress? Denis is waiting for me to point out the house to him and I can't believe it when he actually spots it first. My photos must have been good!

It's a different story when we walk up the path looking for our new house. There is a maze of walkways and steps and I must have taken the wrong path and I have to retrace my steps. I know there is a flight of twenty-seven steps before I turn right as I counted them last time I was here, so I wouldn't get lost. I breathe a big sigh of relief when the house comes into view. For a minute there, I really thought I was lost!

"Izvolite!" (Here it is) I call out to Denis as I gesture towards our house. I have learnt more Croatian. I give Denis the keys and hold my breath, as I wait to see his reaction to our new purchase.

He's very quiet as he wanders around taking it all in and it makes me anxious. Perhaps, he doesn't like it. I'm almost afraid to speak in case he thinks I've bought a lemon.

He exclaims, "I love it!" and now, we are both smiling.

What an adventure we have embarked upon. Where to begin? That's our next decision, but this dilemma is solved very quickly when we discover there is definitely no power or water. We're disappointed, but there is nothing we can do today to solve this immediate problem. Perhaps we can stay at Natasha and Igor's temporarily. After very little deliberation we set off to go and see them.

They are very surprised to see us and even more surprised when we tell them we have bought the 'Silić Fatara' house. They are more than happy for us to stay in the 'hobbit house' when we explain that the house has no power or water. Their tourist bookings for the year have not yet started.

Over the next three weeks we begin the gruelling task of clearing out our house. As there seems to be so much to do, our plan is to clear each room before starting on the next one and once the main house is empty I will begin cleaning and painting. I've never seen so much junk. It's unbelievable. We intend to leave the kitchen for the moment. It's in the 'too hard basket'.

Our neighbour, who we've introduced ourselves to, has kindly agreed to let us use her well or cisterna as they are called here. It's a short-term novelty drawing water using a bucket on the end of a rope and it's not quite what we expected we'd be doing. However, we're grateful, as despite extensive searching we haven't been able to find our water connection. While shopping at the store, we mention our problem to Andrija; he is convinced that we will find it in the garden directly in front of the wine cellar. He is right, there it is buried under soil and rubbish, but, unfortunately, when Denis turns it on only a trickle comes out and we are not able to fix it. Once again Andrija comes to the rescue; the woman who works at Vodavod (the water company) in Korčula lives just around the corner and he will ask her to arrange for it to be fixed. And a couple of days later, we have water. No one has mentioned a water account. Perhaps there are no water rates here. I'm sure we'll find out sooner or later.

With the aid of a mallet, for smashing up the shitty, old furniture, we began to throw out the rubbish. Three canvas sacks left here by the previous owners come in very handy as reusable, rubbish bags and every day we are regular visitors to the rubbish tip. So far, we must have transported about sixty bags and we haven't even started on the dead appliances or the big furniture such as the beds! At the end of every day we are exhausted, dusty and dirty. My entire body aches, my back feels as if it's been destroyed and after showers in the hobbit house, which usually empty the water tank, I just die when my head hits the pillow.

Our lack of power is still a problem; even though I've been to Elektrojug, the power company in Korčula, to see if I can get it connected, I've not been successful. The man in charge is very nice and smiley, but the only word of English he speaks is 'Ok'! When he asks again for a copy of the purchase contract for the house I do my best to explain to him that I have already given it to him, but he can't find it. It must be lost somewhere in the mess of papers on his desk and it is easier just to give him another copy. He is always really busy and his phone rings constantly and no matter what I do, I cannot seem to find out what is holding things up. After three visits to his office I still don't seem to have achieved a thing! Why is it so hard?

It's time to clear the steps leading up to the house; we've both had enough of being slapped in the face by vegetation as we come and go. It turns into a lengthy job; the weeds are so dense it takes me most of the week to slay and dispose of them. But, it's a really worthwhile job and two of the neighbours even come by to express their approval. Within days, the news of our reappearance in the village has spread. Ranko, the man with the bright blue eyes, came over tonight while we were recovering from the day's work on the balcony of the hobbit house to ask if we need a builder. His timing couldn't be better and he agrees to come to our house tomorrow to have a look at the disastrous mess in our kitchen.

We are so pleased. Ranko has agreed to repair the kitchen and he will start in July, immediately after we leave. First of all, he intends to solve our power problem. Apparently, his good friend works for Elektrojug.

Some days later the main bedroom is ready to be painted and we must buy paint from the hardware shop in Korčula. It's our first visit to buy paint and we're astounded to discover that if we want anything other than white paint we must tint it ourselves. They do not mix colours here.

"What you paint? Why you want colour?" We are asked. When we tell the salesman it is for the bedroom. He says,

"You want white. All inside walls are white!" Much to his horror we buy white paint and also two small bottles of tint. We have an attachment on Denis' drill that can mix paint and we will create our own colour. It's not as easy as we thought it would be to get the colour we want, but in the end it turns out ok. Our colour is a rich cream. Ranko also wants to know why we don't use white too. Everyone uses white he says! With a laugh he names our colour 'kiwi white'. We've made a note of our paint recipe as otherwise it is quite possible that every room will end up a different shade.

A house is not a home without a cat and it looks as if we now have a black and white kitten. She comes every afternoon to sleep in the sun in a nest made of grass on the old, stone steps beside the ruin next to our house. She's small and delicate-looking except for her big feet and she has funny black and white markings on her face, a little like an orca whale! She's timid and runs away if I try to pick her up or touch her, but she will drink milk from a saucer as long as I don't get too close to her. Extremely agile and fast, she is quick to catch the turquoise-backed lizards as they bask in the sun on the wall of the ruin. She makes quite a sport of the chase and often the lizard ends up dropping its tail and escaping. Her hunting instinct is strong and though she's very cute, she seems almost wild. I'm sure she must belong to someone and I don't think I should feed her regularly as her owner may become upset.

I've tried to send her home on numerous occasions now, but she simply won't go. The lady next door says she belongs to a little girl who lives close by, but as that house has just acquired a yapping, apricot poodle I wouldn't be surprised if the little black and white cat doesn't like this new addition to the household and has moved out. Having found out about the dog that now lives at her old house, I don't feel bad about feeding her and my mind is made up when the neighbour finishes her story by telling me the cat's name. She's called 'Noosa!' The little girl named her and 'Noosa' is not a Croatian word and no one has any idea what it means. I'd like to spend more time befriending our kitten but, I must press on with my cleaning and painting. Maybe, soon she will let me pick her up.

Our bedroom walls look great with their new coat of paint and now, I'm working on the study. But, I must stop painting, I've been at it for days, my back is too sore and I need a break. I will clean the dirty parquet floors which are encrusted with paint spots, black, sticky stuff, and general dirt. It's a very slow task as I make my way round the floor sitting on an old cushion, scrubbing each room inch by inch with my scraper and steel wool. The mop comes next and finally floor polish. It's tedious and it takes me much longer than I expected it to, but the result is magnificent. The floors are so shiny I can almost see my face in them.

The progress we've made with the painting and the removal of the smaller items of rubbish is going well and today the old fridge and larger items of furniture will be taken to the tip with the help of four school boys from the village and a truck. As Denis begins to move the dead fridge down the steps beside the house, a woman of sixty-plus with vicious, bright, red hair walks past and sees him struggling. Without hesitation, she picks up one end of the fridge as if it's a featherweight and helps him carry it.

We are almost done and now, there is only one large piece of furniture left to be moved. Our school boy helpers are contemplating the old washing machine in the bathroom with much moaning and groaning. Perhaps we should have retained the old woman with the red hair. I'm sure she would have done the job with fewer complaints! The washing machine has a concrete block inside it making it ridiculously heavy. But, after a lot of effort from four people it's finally out of the house and on its way down to the truck. The rubbish is stacked up, waiting to be loaded onto the truck, and I can't believe my eyes when several local scavengers appear and begin rummaging through, looking for treasures! Three old women carry away the chest freezer! The funniest of all, however, is Andrija from the store; he rescues an old, green, lounge chair and places it like a throne outside his shop before beating it severely with a stick! Within minutes he is surrounded by a green cloud of dust! I have never seen scavengers like these village people. However, it suits us fine as now there is more space on the truck. As I watch the truck drive away heading for the tip, I almost feel cleansed.

Over lunch, we've decided to clear the garden which has not been touched for many years. I only need to look at the magnitude of overgrown mess here and I know that this job is too difficult for me and I am reduced to watching. The trellis bordering the terrace on which a grape once grew has fallen to the ground as the timber frame has rotted. The wires are a rusted, tangled mess in amongst the weeds. The leather gloves Denis found in the konoba are a godsend as the rusty wires buried in amongst the giant weeds are rather dangerous. Hopefully, the grape can be saved; it just needs tying back onto the metal frame, which is still intact around the terrace, and pruning at the right time of year. The main grape stem is thicker than my wrist, which must mean it's very old. There are also two rose bushes buried in the garden, which we will try to rescue. Denis does a great job and two days later the garden is at last cleared; the soil looks light and fertile and we think we will plant vegetables here.

Now that we are in gardening mode we've decided to continue and tackle the mess in front of the konoba. As it's the entrance to our property and looks particularly unsightly, we'd really like to clean it up. Unfortunately here, there are some things that we cannot do anything about at the moment. The rotten floor beams lying in front of the konoba are too big and heavy to be moved without first being cut up, and we do not have a saw. The concrete paving is green with mould and though we make some progress removing mould and weeds, at the end of the day, unfortunately, this job is far from finished.

One job that I can easily do is to move the wood that someone has been storing on our land in front of the konoba. It happens to be right where I intend to plant a lavender garden and while I am restacking it on top of a stone wall, out of the way, an old man appears. His eyes are firmly focused on the ground and he looks furtive. He ignores me as he marches across our land to get wood. He doesn't answer when I speak to him and neither does he seem to consider that he might be trespassing. The following day, when he returns, I endeavour to tell him, in Croatian, that he can take the firewood, but he shakes his head and indicates that he doesn't want it and when I try to insist his answer is still 'no'. I really don't understand what's happening here and I conclude that maybe he didn't understand what I was trying to tell him or maybe he is deaf.

Our time here has gone very quickly and already it's late June. The temperature has risen sharply and it's become too hot to work outside in the garden during the middle of the day. Most mornings Denis walks across to our house to spend a couple of hours in the garden before breakfast and today he has returned with an amusing tale. At five o'clock this morning, while he was working in the garden around the back of the house, he heard voices at the front of the house. Looking out of the upstairs window onto the courtyard in front of the konoba, he saw the old man, a wheelbarrow, and two of the secondary school boys who helped load the truck with our rubbish. The boys were loading the last of the firewood into the wheelbarrow under instruction from the old man while he shouted at them to hurry up. I learn later that, at ninety-one, the old man is actually the oldest man in the village.

It's our last night on Korčula and we have booked a table at Konoba Vala for dinner. Denis has gone back to lock our house and make sure the shutters are secure; it won't take him long. I can't face saying goodbye to our house. Already it's under my skin and very much a part of me. Closing up the doors and particularly the shutters, would be just too sad as quite frankly I really don't want to leave. An hour and a half goes by and he still isn't back. I can't ring him as he doesn't have a phone, but I'm starting to get a little concerned and also very hungry. There is nothing to eat here as we are leaving tomorrow and we have let our food supplies run out. Not knowing what else to do to pass the time, I decide to read my book and I've just settled down when I hear heavy footsteps coming up the stairs of the hobbit house. I can't believe it. He is drunk. Apparently, it had got around the village that our departure was imminent so six different people invited Denis in for a farewell drink. They don't take no for an answer here and it is considered rude if you refuse their invitations!

On the way to the airport, as agreed, we will stop off at Boris' office in Dubrovnik to pay the balance of the purchase price. We have reached the outskirts of Dubrovnik when my mobile rings.

"Barbara! This is Dario. Can you hear me?" His voice sounds far away.

"Yes, I can hear you." I can tell by his tone that something is up.

"I'm calling you from the toilet! You must not come to the office until I tell you. Karl has turned up and he says he is here to see you to get his commission. He must have found out from the seller that you were coming here today. But, don't worry; we'll get rid of him. You must park around the corner and I will call you again when the coast is clear!"

A short time later, we are safely ensconced in Boris' office waiting for the vendor to arrive. Dario hasn't mentioned what he and Boris said or did to remove Karl and I have no desire to ask. As far as I'm concerned Karl is simply an obnoxious weed in this Garden of Eden and the time has come to uproot him. There is still no sign of the vendor when Boris receives a telephone call from the vendor's wife. We have a problem. Her husband is still at sea and won't be returning for another two weeks and of course, by then, we will be well and truly back home in Noosa. In Croatia, it is usual for all the parties to be present when the balance of the purchase price is paid, but this has now become impossible. Our only option is to leave our money with Boris for him to settle the purchase, when the vendor finally arrives in Dubrovnik.

Regardless of the happenings in the last couple of days I depart my beloved Croatia knowing that our new house is a very fine house and it will be even better by the time we have finished renovating it.

9
The Transformation

October 2006

We are hoping to get to Korčula before dark. However, as we round the final bend and the wharf at Orebić comes into view, the ferry is pulling away. We have missed it. The winter timetable is operating and it's a long hour and a half wait until the next ferry arrives. Unfortunately, it will be dark by the time we reach Račišće.

The lovely, old, brass lamps on the waterfront in Račišće cast a soft, romantic, glow over the water's edge as we drive into the village and I feel as if I have returned home. The beautiful, old, stone houses welcome me and there in the midst of them is our house still standing proud and tall. We've been invited for dinner by our friends Clare and Tom. The glorious smell of roast pork is issuing from Clare's kitchen as they welcome us with a glass of rakija.

We are eager to see what progress Ranko has made on our house in the months while we have been away. Things are moving well and the house is really coming together. The power is on and the rewiring has been completed. There's a new meter board, lights and power points. The kitchen has been stripped and replastered. Outside, even in the semi-darkness, the huge pile of rubble from the kitchen looms up like a giant, grey ghost. The hot water cylinder in the bathroom has been moved, but is not yet connected. Meteor, the furniture company, whose name really makes me laugh, as their service is so slow it is almost non-existent, have delivered our bed and although they said they would assemble it, they have not. Our house is looking much more habitable, but it's still not quite ready for us to move in and after a fabulous dinner of roast pork and apple crumble we accept our friends' invitation to stay with them for a few days.

It's all happening today! The man from Elektrojug has come to connect the hot water. Denis is sitting on the floor surrounded by a hundred screws of all sizes and instructions – in Croatian – as he assembles our bed. It's a slow process, but two hours later after much grumbling and grizzling, it is finished.

The first night in our new house and it's too silent, I can't sleep. The bed is warm and cosy, but it's the quietest environment I have ever been in at night. When I close my eyes the only sound I can hear is the ticking of my watch!

As the days pass, Ranko continues to work on our simple, new kitchen. Today, he has built a magnificent stone bench for our espresso machine using a hundred-year-old slab of stone from the ruin next door. The shiny Italian espresso machine will look superb in its new home. His progress on our kitchen is rapid; tomorrow he will begin to tile the kitchen bench and install our gas cooktop. With the kitchen almost ready for use I must go to Elektrojug again, this time to establish a power account. Although Ranko succeeded in getting the power reconnected and the initial reconnection fee has been paid, the account is still not in my name. We've been using power since the beginning of July; it's October now, and as yet I haven't received a bill. This time, I finally get to the bottom of it. Elektrojug will not issue me with an account as the previous owner has not cancelled his account or the automatic payment from his bank despite requests from Elektrojug and my solicitor. I can only assume that the account for the last three months has been paid by him! At the moment, there is nothing further I can do except wait until he cancels his account and hope that the power is not cut off in the interim.

Still reeling from our discoveries at Elektrojug, we arrive home to a surprise. Having finished the kitchen, Ranko has begun work on the back wall of the house next to the terrace. Chipping off the old discoloured plaster he has exposed the magnificent stone underneath. The transformation is amazing. Next, he will remove the old grout with a special tool before replacing it with new grout. This job takes patience and skill, but Ranko absolutely loves this work and with his artistic eye he does a brilliant job. I can't believe that they covered such lovely stones with plaster; but, apparently, this was the fashion in the 1950s. If you plastered your house it was considered a sign of wealth.

Eager to get the interior of the house liveable, Denis and I are both painting now. I'm working on the interior stair rail which will be shiny black and Denis is painting the ceilings in our bedroom and my study. We are slowly becoming used to the paint here. It is very different to paint in New Zealand and Australia with its odd, chalky consistency; however, it's cheap and no doubt it's been designed for the stone walls here. At the end of the day, stiff and tired from painting, I love to wander around my garden. All the garden areas are doing well and most of the plants have survived the hot summer. The boy next door – Curly, as we call him, on account of his thick, unruly, mass of dark, blond curls, did a great job of watering them over the last three months, in our absence. Today, I've come across three, giant, silverbeet plants that have self-seeded in the vegetable garden. They are such a lovely everlasting reminder of my childhood and I'm looking forward to eating them. The herb gardens we planted in the old ship's boiler next to the vegetable garden and along the back path are growing quickly and we have already begun to pick them. They thrive in the climate here as I would never have believed. The leaves on the sage plants are huge and the flowers in spring a deep, intense blue. Rosemary bushes seem to double in size almost overnight and our oregano and mint have already grown into giant specimens. The basil is so lush that I am able to make lavish quantities of pesto using walnuts and a superb local parmesan. Never before have I had such a magnificent healthy selection of herbs in my garden. I'm convinced that if there is a herb heaven then it must be here.

There is only one problem in my garden and it's in my lavender patch in front of the konoba. The biggest plant on the end has a ring of rusty nails pushed in the ground in a circle around the stem and as fast as I fill in the big hole that keeps appearing behind it, it reappears! It will only be a matter of time before it dies. I wonder who is trying to kill it and why?

I'm about to use my Croatian washing machine for the first time. What a strange looking thing it is. Normal on the outside, but inside there is a cage that you put the clothes in and clip shut. Fortunately, it has English instructions. It works ok, but doesn't spin the clothes very well at the end of the cycle and there is a lot of water left in them. I guess I'll get used to it and as it's as windy as Wellington today drying should be fine. I'm very happy to be able to finally wash my own clothes. When we were staying at Natasha and Igor's house, Natasha very kindly did the washing for me and it didn't occur to me to ask whether she would wash them in cold or hot water. When she returned the clothes to me sparkling white and beautifully ironed I believed she'd done a brilliant job until I put them on. She had boiled them to death and they had shrunk several sizes! Apparently, everyone here washes in ridiculously, hot water as they believe you cannot use cold as the clothes will not be washed properly! The other source of humour here is washing day in the house around the corner. This only happens about once every three weeks and when it does there are rows and rows of white Jockey 'Y' fronts hanging on the line.

Several of the villagers have seen Ranko working on the back of the house and come to have a look. At first, I thought that they were here to admire and compliment him on his job, but they had come to express their opinions in no uncertain terms. They are very outspoken here and don't hesitate to tell you what they think. Ranko is using pale-coloured grout to match the stone, but the locals think the grout should be dark grey and don't hesitate to say so.

The painting in the upstairs of the house and the stairwell is almost finished and it's time for a break – a morning shopping in Korčula. The kitchen is now finished also and once we equip it, we can use it. We don't need a lot, mostly pots and pans as we intend to use many of the previous owners' things, including the dinner set from Poland. There is a well-stocked, kitchen shop in Korčula where we buy an inexpensive, good quality set of Italian, stainless steel pots, pans and cutlery.

Now, that the painting in the interior of the house is almost finished, the kitchen table and chairs are next on my list of jobs. The existing ones are old and as there is nothing wrong with them I intend to bring them back to life with a coat of olive-green paint and I will recover their seats with a hard-wearing green and cream fabric.

As he has finished replacing the grout in the back wall Ranko has now decided he wants to see what's in the attic; he's hoping for treasure, he says. There's no gold, but there is a two hundred-year-old, hand-painted, sea chest. It's a bit battered, but worth salvaging as it will be a useful for storage.

As always our time here has gone too quickly and already it's the end of November. The temperature has dropped several degrees and rain and wind have arrived. It's the bura, a cold, dry wind from the north – autumn is here and the plants in the garden are not happy. Their leaves are turning brown and shrivelling almost before my eyes. For me also, it's too cold to continue painting my chairs; I've been working on the terrace in the sun, but now that the sun has gone the atmosphere is too damp for my paint to dry.

Ranko has unearthed another treasure, this time it's in the konoba; a huge, stone vessel (kamenića) that was once used to hold olive oil. Carved from one piece of stone, it's an impressive monster. Ranko, Denis and a couple of helpers move it outside the konoba and position it underneath the existing trellis. I will use it as a planter box for herbs and a grape.

Almost every house has a kamenića in the konoba which was probably hand carved by a member of the family. Most of these vessels hold 200 litres of olive oil, but some are ridiculously huge and can hold as much as 1,500 litres. In the days gone by, if you didn't own a kamenića and you wanted to buy one then the payment for someone to carve one for you would have been the amount of olive oil that the vessel could contain.

Wine is still stored by some households in their konobas in stone amphorae. These beautiful, old vessels are mostly oval shaped with handles on each side and a lid that fits as snug as the lid on a teapot. Like the kamenićas, these too have been hand carved and are also extremely heavy. A lid alone can weigh as much as forty kilos.

In the last few years there have been instances of these valuable vessels being stolen during the night by thieves in speed boats and taken to Europe where they are sold for large sums of money.

Today, it's another shopping trip to Korčula. I enjoy buying things here as most of the prices are a lot lower than New Zealand. One of the items on today's list is weed-killer; the weeds on the back path are out of control. Though we've tried, we haven't been able to find the Croatian word for weed killer and as the man in the garden shop speaks absolutely no English we cannot make him understand what we want to buy. We are about to give up when a new customer, who speaks English and Croatian, comes in. The Croatian word for weed-killer is some unpronounceable mouthful, but luckily he knows it!

Laden with weed killer and other items from the hardware store, which Ranko has asked us to buy, we arrive home to discover him being verbally assaulted by 'old man wood stealer's' wife. Over eighty, with her hair dyed jet black, wearing all black, including thick, black stockings, she is seriously formidable. She screams at Ranko as she stamps her walking stick repeatedly on the ground. She has an unusual accent and I can't understand a word she says. Ranko tolerates her for a short time until she obviously says something that offends him and suddenly his blue eyes flash and he shouts back at her. Within seconds a fierce slanging match erupts between them until she gives a final stab of her walking stick and storms off. I have been hiding in the kitchen! She is altogether too scary for me. It seems she has been complaining about my lavender plant. She thinks it's too close to her wall! When Ranko tells her it's our land and we can do what we like with it, she responds by telling him that we should go back where we came from. That's when Ranko loses his temper and points out to her that she is not even from this village. She comes from Cavtat near Dubrovnik! After this outburst, we know that either she or her husband must come in the dead of night to dig the hole behind the lavender plant and put the nails in the ground.

After the episode with our lavender plant we now totally believe the stories we have heard from the German couple who own a holiday home here. Not long after they bought their house at the other end of the village, the old lady next door made it clear that she did not like them when she poisoned their fully grown orange tree and subsequently cut it down. Although the incident was common knowledge around the village no one said a word to the old lady. The German couple were advised that they should not report it to the police as that is not done here! Next, grapes the couple had just planted were ripped out in the dead of night and thrown away.

Feeling dispirited about their garden Inga and Hans decided to turn their attention to repainting their newly acquired boat. They had chosen dark green paint and no sooner had they begun the job when a group of locals turned up and began to stare. Immediately after Hans had applied the first few strokes of paint, one of the locals appeared, eager to have his say.

"Bah! Why you paint it green. Green is the colour of Turska! We don't paint green here. You must change the colour." Hans ignored him until finally the man who had spoken out scoffed, stormed off and was closely followed by the rest of the meddling clan.

Ranko seems unconcerned at the abuse he has received and shrugs it off, saying that they are a grumpy, old couple who have nothing better to do than complain constantly. Apparently, he had a job near their house last year working on scaffolding and the old lady developed a habit of standing underneath the scaffolding and shouting at him incessantly! He ignored her until eventually she gave up and went away.

Today Ranko has bought us a present. It's one of the local delicacies; a piece of pršut (dried smoked ham) that has been smoked by one of his friends in Blato. It's tasty and has a lovely, strong, smoky flavour.

There's no work for us as today, November 1 is a holiday. It's All Saints Day. The flower shops and garden centres have been full of chrysanthemums for days. In remembrance of my family, we've made a wreath, to take to the cemetery, using wild flowers and roses from our garden. People come and go from the cemetery all day long and at the end of the day it's full of fresh flowers and it's a particularly beautiful sight.

It's now mid-November and overnight the weather has suddenly turned to winter with temperatures of five degrees at night and a mere twelve during the day. Ranko and Denis have cleaned the chimney and Ranko intends to light our wood-fired oven for the first time in thirty years! He is adamant that *he* must light it. However, Denis is impatient and can't wait and goes ahead and lights it without Ranko. Within five minutes the kitchen is full of thick, choking, black smoke. It's so bad we are forced to go outside as we are having difficulty breathing.

"I told you to wait. You must do as I say. It's not like normal fire. You must know what you are doing. Auf! Look at the smoke!" Ranko shakes his head and although his voice is stern he is laughing at Denis and so am I! I knew there had to be a reason why Ranko told him to wait. He doesn't talk just for the sake of talking.

Once you know how to light the oven, it works well for cooking and heating the kitchen. I'm reluctant to work outside now, as it's so toasty and warm in the big kitchen. For dinner we have just eaten a superb chicken casserole cooked on top of the old stove. The chicken here is extremely good and I've combined it with onions, lemon slices, our own plump, fat, juicy olives, thyme and white wine. It's great; a flavoursome meal cooked in our le Creuset cast-iron casserole dish. I'm really glad we decided to keep the oven and not replace it with a heater.

All that remains, to more or less complete the kitchen, is to clean the floor and put up the pantry shelves. Until now, I have resisted trying to remove the lime and cement from the terrazzo tiles on the floor. It's not something I'm used to dealing with and quite frankly I really don't know what to use to clean them. It seems that Ranko knows how to deal with the mess coating the tiles and he arrives one morning with vinegar to neutralise the lime. It's a nasty job grovelling on the floor and scrubbing it, but the vinegar cuts through the lime easily and a scraper does the rest. The tiles look great and once again I'm pleased we decided to keep and restore them.

Shortly, we must return to Australia, but before we go, having completed a good amount of work on our house, we'd like to begin to enjoy some of the seasonal happenings in the village. In a few days, olive harvest will begin and Denis is very happy to have been invited by Igor and Natasha to help them pick their crop. I'm exempt as I have injured my knee; however, they have very kindly invited me for lunch in the olive grove.

In Račišće, olive picking doesn't start until the dew has dried. Today, four, large, olive trees will be picked; tarpaulins and nets are spread out underneath to catch the fruit and ladders are propped for access to the upper branches. Igor's extended family, who have arrived from as far away as Split and Rijeka, are here today to help. Olive harvest is a real family get-together, almost like a reunion that happens once a year. People arrive from as far afield as New Zealand and Australia to help with their families' harvest. It's an amazingly social time, perhaps even more social than Christmas.

Once the tarpaulin is full, traditionally the olives are stalked and the leaves removed on the ground under the trees. As this is uncomfortable back-breaking work, often the olives are transported home in plastic bags where, in the cool of the evening, they are put on slotted racking tables in the konoba where the stalks and leaves are removed without the necessity of grovelling on the ground. This is a much easier method and definitely does away with back ache. We believe it is essential to remove both the stalks and the leaves before pressing as in our experience, even a small proportion of these can add bitterness to the oil.

Today, there is no wind and although it's autumn, it's still warm enough to sit outside and enjoy the watery sun. Igor has made a grill using last year's, dried, olive branch clippings. On the menu there are chops, sausages, chicken, coleslaw and bread washed down with red wine from Lumbarda. It is quite a feast to partake in, underneath the olive trees. Igor and Natasha are delightful, hospitable people and I had almost forgotten how much I enjoy their company.

Tomorrow is a rest day and on Wednesday, two large trees, which are heavily laden with fruit, will be picked. These trees were planted by Igor's great grandfather over three hundred years ago and they promise to be spectacular. Sitting on a rock in the olive grove amongst these spectacular old, olive trees and the ancient stone walls, I can't resist crushing a couple of olives in my palm and rubbing the oil into my hands which are very dry from painting and gardening. What a great treat for my hands as they suck up the oil quickly and feel like silk.

On Wednesday, it takes Igor, Natasha and Denis all day to strip the two, huge trees. I have come along merely to take photos and soak up the atmosphere. The chat during picking is mostly about olives and grapes. Size and quality are always discussed and if the people in the grove next door are also picking then the conversation is often loud and animated as the village people boast about their own particular harvests.

The family in the adjacent grove, which includes a very old lady, are intrigued to find Denis, a foreigner, helping Igor and Natasha pick and they can't help shouting out across the ancient stone wall to find out who Denis is and why he is here. Igor gives them a run-down on my family and how I fit into the village and the old lady responds by saying she knew my family a long time ago. As interested and helpful as they are unfortunately I do not gain any new information about any living relatives.

Today, there is yet another grill for lunch and this time it's chicken schnitzel, tomato, paprika and cabbage salad, lightly battered, little fish and of course bread and wine. During lunch Denis is presented with a kilo of black olives as a thank you for helping out and Igor invites us to the village press on Saturday night to watch the pressing of their olives.

Once the picking is finished we leave Igor with his pruning saw and secateurs. He will now complete the annual prune of what is one of the best cared for, most productive groves in the village.

On our walk home we learn that two people have been hurt today while picking. One fell from the fork of a tree and the other fell off a ladder. Thankfully, neither person has been badly injured and although Denis is exhausted after his hard day's work and is very much looking forward to a hot shower to ease his aching back, he is at least, in one piece.

The calm weather is gone now and the bura has begun to blow. It's so cold, it reminds me once again of Wellington. Today, Ranko is taking us to his hometown, Blato, for us to order an outdoor table and seats for our terrace. His friend Karlo, who has a wood working business, will make them. As this will be our first trip to Blato, Ranko suggests we take what he calls the scenic route through the less populated part of the island. The coastline here is more rugged and the houses are minimal; quite different to the coast of Korčula where our village is situated. Not long after we begin our journey the roadside is transformed with multitudes of pretty, wild flowers.

Huge bright, pink thistles, pink and red hollyhocks and yarrow are all flourishing in a wonderfully natural, unspoilt environment.

Darkness is falling as we descend the steep hillside leading into Blato, one of the largest towns on Korčula. Stone houses with twinkling lights, sit in clusters facing each other on the surrounding hillsides. On the flat, at the entrance to Blato, the road turns into a tree-lined tunnel with zlinj (lime) trees growing along both sides of it. They remind me of the jacaranda trees in Harare. Apparently, these limes trees flower in summer and give off a strong perfume. I'd love to see them then, they must be spectacular.

The people in Blato have a different appearance. Many of the men wear ties and berets and generally seem more formally dressed than the men in our village. Push bikes are popular here and the combination of berets and bikes makes it reminiscent of a French village.

Blato has a very well-stocked hardware store where we happily purchase several items, including paint. Unlike Korčula, this shop will mix our chosen colours for us! As we leave the hardware store the owner calls out jokingly to Denis,

"Now remember your paint is called 101!"

Our shopping is finished and Ranko intends to cook a 'grill' for dinner at Karlo's house. The butcher's shop is our next stop. Ranko is buying pork and chicken when Denis points to a different meat on display and asks him what it is. Ranko hesitates. He can't think of the English word.

"Big chicken. Pork!" He says, meaning turkey. From then on it becomes a joke between us, 'Pigs can fly!' There are capers for sale here too and Ranko adds them to his shopping list. Soon, he will make us his octopus salad.

At Karlo's house, in the back streets, we are greeted by a small, barking dog and two rough-looking men who turn out to be Karlo and his son Lazar. They're busy loading plastic bags full of olives on to a trailer in readiness for taking them to the press. These olives are much smaller than the ones in our village and I'm told they are a different variety. Apparently,

Račišće has its own particular variety, different from the ones in other villages on the island.

Once the introductions are over, we follow Karlo into his konoba, which is now his work shop, and unexpectedly find ourselves knee deep in wood shavings! The place is never cleaned and there is so much sawdust everywhere that it's difficult to walk. Even the cobwebs hanging from the lights are coated with it. It's so hilarious it looks like a film set and I find myself half expecting a ghost to emerge from a dark corner. Having confirmed the dimensions of the table and the delivery date, we return upstairs to the living room for a drink while Ranko begins his preparations for the grill. Ranko's friend Karlo and his son remind me of cartoon characters. Karlo is a thin bohemian with grey, scraggly hair and a beard and Lazar who is even thinner than his father, is quite ugly and has a bony face that does nothing to enhance his looks. His limp, oily hair looks like it smells and his clothes, which are unclean, hang off him. Quite clearly, they are bachelors. Not only their appearance, but the state of their house reflects this. Ranko has trouble finding a space on the bench to do the preparation for the meal and I will be surprised if there are any clean plates for dinner as there are so many dirty ones piled up on the bench! However, they are friendly, relaxed and hospitable in their own peculiar fashion.

Ranko lights the fire for the grill while we sit around the living room table drinking wine and chatting about Karlo's work. As well as woodworking, he also paints and used to do iron work and stone carving. There are various examples of his talent or in some cases, lack of it, around the room. Lazar can't wait to show Denis the painting of a nun smacking a bare bottom lying across her knees! It's funny if a little naive and out of proportion. Karlo's iron work and carving show more promise, especially the stone carving of 'St somebody or rather.' It's been very well done.

While talking to Lazar, Denis, who often has a tendency towards verbal diarrhoea, begins bombarding Lazar with too much chat at too fast a pace. Lazar becomes totally lost in the conversation, turns to Denis with an exasperated look on his face and blurts out,

"Are you fucking with me?" His voice is slurred and when Denis doesn't reply he repeats himself even more loudly. This time Denis gets such a shock it leaves him speechless. Lazar does speak English, but tonight his words are almost incoherent and he is clearly under the influence of either drugs or alcohol, which Ranko tells us he indulges in so heavily that his brain is now somewhat dead! As uncouth as he is, I can't help but find him humorous.

Next, the conversation turns to me and my roots. Denis tries, but fails to explain, in Croatian, that five generations of my family have lived in Račišće. Unknowingly, he actually says that *I* am three hundred years old! Everyone laughs and the awkward moment is soon forgotten as Ranko brings the grilled meat to the table. Dinner is ready.

Ranko's food is good. The meat is tender and smoky and Karlo adds to the selection on the table with raw onion (which I do not eat) pickled paprika and green olives. The olives have been roasted and then put in brine. I find them too salty, almost unpleasant, but the others appear to enjoy them.

It's a forty-minute drive back to our village and time to go. Blato sits at a much higher altitude than Račišće and as you would expect it's very cold outside. Mist is beginning to envelope the village as we make our way back to the car. It's eerily silent as we pick our way through the maze of alleyways under the dim street lights. Our path takes us past the house where Ranko was born and spent his childhood. From the outside, it looks particularly old and even though it's small, there are two ornate, carved, stone pillars at its entrance. As we admire his house, Ranko tells us that when he was a child so many people were crammed into it that the only space left for him to sleep, was in a small bed underneath the stairwell leading to the attic.

Back in our village the following day, we are hoping the weather will hold for Ranko to finish laying the tiles on our terrace and concreting the back path. We must at least finish resealing the terrace to prevent the winter rain damaging our newly completed kitchen. It turns into a race against the weather as Ranko and Denis work furiously in the face of the bura which we know is on its way. Heavy rain arrives together with the bura, but we are lucky both jobs are finished.

On Saturday night, just before eight, we walk over to Igor's and Natasha's place. We have been invited for a drink before we accompany them to the olive press. A phone call lets us know the press has been exceptionally busy and as it's running behind schedule, Igor's pressing has been delayed for an hour and a half. To fill in time, Natasha makes a snack for us. It's a popular Croatian dessert – palačinke (crepes) filled with jam. She serves them with Igor's prošec (dessert wine) made in 2003. It's an absolutely irresistible combination.

A hive of activity is going on inside and outside the tatty, old building that houses the village olive press; people are coming and going with olives and oil. The wonderfully, warm building is heated by a homemade furnace that uses spent olive crushings as fuel. Locals gather in groups, chatting as they wait for their turn at the press. The blazing furnace is looked after by a cripple we have seen around the village and although he looks happy enough, the beginning of his life was tragic and I feel sad whenever I see him. He was born after his mother tried unsuccessfully to abort him. As this is a catholic village, abortion was not available at the time of his conception and she took it upon herself to try to abort him by her own means. Sadly, he was born retarded and slightly crippled. It makes me happy to see how important he feels having been given the job of fire tender, even if he does choke the fire with too many green, olive crushings and cause it to blow back! The atmosphere is warm and friendly and no one pays any attention when, from time to time the air is punctuated with a loud boom as the door of the furnace flies open and it belches flames and black smoke!

During the day, this poor man has another job he loves. He lives in the neighbouring village of Kneže and at twelve noon each day he rings the church bells to mark the time. He can't actually tell the time, but he knows that when both the hands of the clock point straight up at the same time, he must ring the bell. When he forgets, as he often does, he still rings the bell even if it is too late!

At other times of the year, we see him engaged in odd jobs around the village such as helping to put the chairs and tables in front of the hotel. People are generally mindful of his disabilities and often shout him an alcohol free beer at either the hotel or Konoba Vala.

Fortunately, there are very few disabled people who live in Račišće. The only other one we see, on the waterfront near his house, is an unmarried, stooped, sullen man who walks slowly and deliberately. Rumour has it that he was hit on the head with a rock by a woman during some sort of domestic dispute. As to whether or not this is true remains a mystery, but it is obvious that he suffers from something more than just 'the depression'.

Rich, thick, green oil dribbles out from beneath the mammoth press and I am so mesmerised by it that I can't tear myself away and by the time I do it's quite late, but we both agree the olive pressing has been a marvellous experience.

Olive harvest has finished for this year and I have decided to have one last try at finding out more information about my ancestors. I've put the word out to see if anyone knows anything which could help me and, finally, some new information has come to light. Today we're going to look at the house that was once owned by my great grandfather.

The friendly, existing owner is very proud to show off her house and tells me that her grandmother bought it from my great grandfather just before he left for New Zealand. The house has been altered considerably over the years, but the original roof line is still visible and it's quite clear how small the house was back in 1900. At least six people were crowded into one small room with a lean-to attached to it. I find it impossible to imagine living like this. After she has showed us around, Maria, who is actually our friend Tom's aunt, insists that we share a glass of wine with her and as we do she proposes a toast to my family.

The bura has gone, replaced by several days of crisp fine weather giving Ranko just enough time to complete the addition of a rustic, stone seat underneath our bedroom window. The thick, magnificent slab of stone that forms the actual seat was buried in the garden. We've named it the '*barney*' seat as it looks like something from the *'Flintstones.'* Ranko has done such an outstanding job of the seat that it looks as if it has been there forever. The occasion calls for a photo and I insist that Denis and Ranko (alias Fred and Barney), pose sitting on the seat each holding a Karlovačko (local) beer.

We have one week before it is time to go and it brings on a spurt of energy from both of us. Denis paints the exterior doors and shutters the traditional red oxide and I feel a great sense of achievement when I finish recovering the seats on my kitchen chairs. When rain keeps us indoors I content myself with making marmalade from our plentiful crop of lemons and storing our black olives in brine once they been roasted or treated with salt. We are experimenting with two different methods to preserve them and we will see which method we prefer. Luckily, I have sufficient time to complete one last job – painting the downstairs spare bedroom and cleaning the parquet floor. We have ordered another bed from our favourite furniture shop, Meteor, for delivery after we leave. Family are beginning to make noises about visiting us here soon.

On the day before our departure my last treat is to plant a row of French lavender along the back path. It's a perfect site for them in the stony ground and I am confident they will do well. The purple flowers should look amazing in front of the ancient stone wall.

On our way to the airport in Dubrovnik, I pay one last visit to Elektrojug in Korčula to see if there has been any progress with the power account. But, the man in charge is out and I am confronted by an officious woman who begins to abuse me as soon as I open my mouth to speak. She says she has done so much to help me and that I'm ungrateful and still haven't given her a copy of the purchase contract for the house! I have no idea what I've done to deserve this treatment. She is so scary and hostile that I retreat with assurances that I will fax it to her. This will be the third copy I've given them. Exasperating! Will it ever get sorted and more importantly will our power get cut off?

Recipes

Olives in Brine

1 kg fresh ripe black olives
salt
olive oil

Place washed olives in a non-corrosive dish, sprinkle heavily with coarse salt and mix well. Next day drain away accumulated liquid. Add another sprinkling of salt and leave to marinate. Repeat the procedure for five days. On the sixth day rinse the olives well in a few changes of water.

Brine

100 gm salt per litre of water

Bring water to the boil and add salt. Stir until dissolved. Pack olives into jar with hot brine and thin covering of oil on top. Seal for minimum of four months.

After four months or longer drain and rinse olives then store in olive oil with garlic, lemon, rosemary to suit taste. Store in fridge.

Olive and Lemon Chicken

2 large cloves of garlic
sprigs of thyme
3 sliced lemons
8 chicken pieces
15 black olives
80ml olive oil
2 tbsp lemon juice

Bruise garlic and thyme in mortar with pestle. Add lemon juice and olive oil. Place lemon slices on base of casserole dish, add chicken in a single layer and pour over garlic mixture. Season with salt and pepper and turn to coat. Stand 1 hour. Then add olives.

Preheat oven to 200°C. Roast 20–30 minutes or until chicken is cooked through.

House at the time of purchase, 2006.

House after renovation.

View of the village from road leading into it.

View of village from back road.

View of bay from bedroom window.

Wine cellar, 2006.

10
Winter

February 2007

Denis is going to Račišće for three weeks where he will work with Ranko to make more valuable improvements to our property. I will remain in Noosa as in the past few weeks we have had several changes of staff in Costa Noosa Espresso, including a new manager, and one of us must be there to oversee the day-to-day running of the business.

Ranko has driven to Dubrovnik to pick up Denis and he is very amused to see Denis waiting for him outside the airport in shorts and a t-shirt. Denis seems to have forgotten it's mid-winter in Europe.

Upon his arrival back at in Račišće, Denis is delighted to see that Ranko has already started to strip the old plaster off the front of our house. Once he has exposed the stone he will re-grout it, the same as he did the back. The front face of the house is three storeys high and as it's a large area, working from the scaffolding he has erected, it will take him about six weeks to complete. Not unexpectedly, it's cold in Račišće and

Denis lights the fire every evening to keep warm. Apparently, the little black and white cat has become friendlier now and plucked up the courage to climb onto the bed where she has discovered the furry blanket. When Denis puts her out at night; she is reluctant to go and nips his hand in protest!

Back in Noosa, Karl has been harassing me by email. He is still under the mistaken impression that I owe him commission even though he has already been paid by the vendor. He is trying to '*double dip*' as we call it in New Zealand. I have no contract with him and I definitely do not owe him anything. I had thought that Karl had been weeded out, roots and all, but obviously I was mistaken. He appears to be one very persistent noxious weed in the Garden of Eden. So far, I have responded politely to his emails, hoping he will give up and go away. This time I write him a much stronger reply, which works, and thankfully I do not hear from him again.

As they need more exterior house paint and small hardware items, Denis and Ranko visit the hardware shop in Blato. They enter the store and Ranko attempts to reintroduce Denis to the owner, but he is cut off before he can finish speaking when the owner looks at Denis and says,

"I know you. You are 101!" Denis has a new nickname now. While searching the hardware store for some screws, Denis comes across an absolute bargain – a red waterproof coat on sale for $20NZ, it will be excellent for him to wear while he is water blasting the exterior of the house.

Unbeknown to Denis, Ranko has ordered a present for him and it is now ready to be picked up. It's a handcrafted axe for cutting firewood. Denis emails me a photo of himself wearing the red coat and holding the axe. It's very funny indeed and I rename him the 'Axe Murderer of Račišće!'

Workmen offering to sandblast house roofs have arrived in the village and Denis hires them. The tiles clean up well and are restored to their original terracotta colour. In the photo Denis sends me they look like new. Unfortunately, a huge amount of sand has come into the house around the window frames and made quite a mess. Denis seems concerned, but I'm sure it's nothing the vacuum cleaner can't fix.

Along with the bright, red roof we also have new, copper downpipes to replace the existing ones, which were old and broken. These handmade copper ones really finish off the exterior of the house and give it character, a little like eyebrows on a face.

Word has got around the village that Denis is here on his own and he receives a dinner invitation from Danijel, whose father did the electrical work on our house. Gnocchi is on the menu and Denis arrives early just in time to watch Danijel making it. He has already made the meat sauce earlier in the day. Bag after bag of flour goes into the mixture. Horrified at the quantity of flour he is using Denis suggests that maybe it's enough. But Danijel insists the recipe calls for more and he continues adding it! It comes as no surprise to Denis that the gnocchi end up as heavy as lead and although Denis tries to get away with eating only a small amount of them, Danijel won't take no for an answer and persists in loading up his plate! The village mayor is a little quicker with his reaction and after trying only a couple of mouthfuls he puts his plate on the kitchen bench and declares that he's not hungry! Walking home after dinner Denis feels as if there is a lead weight in his stomach.

In Noosa I've received a fantastic email from Boris. My Croatian citizenship has been granted. Nine months is all it has taken! I will be able to pick up my 'Domovnica' certificate next time I am in Dubrovnik.

The next morning there is snow on the hills of the mainland. The temperature has plummeted overnight in Račišće. The weather is freezing as Denis and Ranko begin working on repairs to the exterior shutters. It's a good time to inspect them now as they are accessible from Ranko's scaffolding. It seems that they are in very bad shape and it must be years since they were last repaired, if ever. Ranko removes and repairs them before Denis stains them with red oxide, the same as the doors.

On Sunday morning Denis was hoping to sleep in, but there is a knock at the door and Ranko arrives with a pig slung over his shoulder. It's time to christen our smoke house.

Ranko and Denis scour the immediate area, including the ruin next door and also the crumbling donkey houses close by, for dry wood to use for the fire underneath the spit. Within a short space of time their yield is sufficient to do the job and while Ranko chops wood and drinks his first beer at nine o'clock in the morning, the chef arrives to supervise the roasting of the pig. When the chef too drinks his first beer, Denis knows the party has already started. 'Big Foot', the chef, is a giant of a man who, considering his size, is surprisingly shy and gentle. Still unmarried at the age of sixty-two, he lives at home with his elderly mother and father. Everyone in the village knows him. He's famous for his cooking skills and the tripe recipe served for breakfast in the hotel, is named after him. Ranko and the chef have wired the pig onto the spit when Ranko realises that there will not be sufficient seating for all of the guests and he sets to work making extra seats from builder's planks and wine barrels.

Three hours later, thirteen people, including our friends Tom and Clare, are squeezed around the kitchen table for a fabulous, winter feast of antipasto, roast pork, potato and kupus salad, bread and wine.

The atmosphere is jovial and the language a mixture of English and Croatian. With most of the renovations now complete, to Denis, this really feels like a housewarming. Amid much laughter, large quantities of alcohol are consumed along with enormous portions of roast pork. Towards the end of the gargantuan meal, Denis receives a lesson in cheese cutting. Apparently the chef is also considered to be an expert in this too. According to 'Big Foot', when cheese is cut into slices they must be exactly 5mm thick – no more and no less!

Feeling very fat and satisfied the guests begin to leave. Denis produces 'doggie' bags of pork for everyone to take home causing copious quantities of laughter to break out.

Before he leaves Denis has one last job to complete, a job especially for me. He's painting the bathroom and making minor improvements to it with new lights, a mirror and a glass shelf. At some point we will need to replace the strange shaped, small bath and also the hot water cylinder which is rusty, but for now these basic improvements will be fine.

This winter the weather in the village has been particularly clear and fine. A below average rainfall and lots of sunny days have enabled Denis to be very satisfied with the tasks he and Ranko have completed on the exterior of our house. If we ever decide to experience a complete winter here it would be wonderful if it was as mild as this one, but somehow I doubt that it would be.

11
Mrs Nasty and Other Horribles

From now on we have decided to make Račišće our main home. Our business, Costa Noosa Espresso, which was not actually for sale, has been sold. Someone knocked on our door and made us an offer we couldn't refuse. We have also sold our house in Noosa Springs and arranged, with great difficulty, for our possessions to be shipped to Croatia. I know it's the other side of the world, but I'm still surprised removal companies seem to know very little about shipping things there, let alone where it actually is! The container is due to arrive in Split by the end of September.

On the afternoon when we arrive back in Račišće, there is a surprise waiting for us in the fridge. Ranko has made his long-talked-about octopus salad for our dinner. He has been talking about it for so long I had begun to think he would never make it! The ingredients are octopus, tomatoes, red onion, potatoes, capers, olive oil and red wine vinegar. The octopus is incredibly tender and I'm sure it has everything to do with being frozen before he cooks it. Denis and I both agree it's the best we have ever tasted. Ranko offers to show me how to make it and I believe I will take him up on his offer. There's also an aged bottle of red wine on the table and I can't help thinking how lovely it is to arrive here and find dinner already cooked and the hot water turned on. The flight was long and as usual we are exhausted and suffering from jet lag.

Now, as the majority of the renovation work has been completed we plan to relax and slow down. The only pressing thing I must do now my Croatian citizenship has been granted, is apply for my osobna iskaznica (Croatian identity card).

Long awaited mail has arrived for us while we've been away. There is a bill from Vodavod (the water company), which is in my name and also a bill from Elektrojug, but this bill is not in my name. It's still in the previous owner's name and it does not go back to the date I purchased the property. The free power is certainly a bonus after all the grief I've been through with the power company. At least it's some progress, but I can't help wondering how many years it will be before the account is transferred into my name.

Our first few days have been spent relaxing and settling in; today we will visit the police station in Korčula where I will apply for my ID card. Dario assures me it will be a straightforward procedure and once I have lodged the application, the card should come in about three weeks. I've been waiting for over an hour in the queue and when I finally reach the front of it, unfortunately, the nondescript woman who assesses the applications turns out be an unhelpful pain in the neck. She is extremely sour and surly as she instructs me to go and pay for the application by buying tax 'stamps' at the local newsagent. The police station issues identity cards, passports and car registration and when I return it is very busy, another queue has developed and I must wait once again. This time she goes through my papers with a fine tooth comb. Her attitude is beginning to make me feel as if I am a criminal! In a gloating voice she announces that one document is missing. She is demanding a certified copy of my birth certificate together with a translation into Croatian. This is totally unreasonable and when I explain to her that I have already provided this for my citizenship application she turns even nastier. I know she is fully aware that this isn't something I can magic up overnight as it must come from New Zealand and it takes time. The ugly smirk on her face tells me she's getting great enjoyment out of asking me for something I can't easily provide. What can I do? I decide to call Dario and get him to talk sense into her. She shrugs indifferently when I hand her the phone and ask her to talk to him. Middle-aged and frumpy, she has a permanent scowl on her face and I doubt she even knows how to smile. As her conversation with Dario continues she will not budge and the scowl on her face turns into yet another a nasty smirk! The papers from my citizenship application are locked in the vault in the police station in Zagreb, but Dario thinks he can get access to them. He has a legal colleague in Zagreb who he believes can get them out and bring them to Korčula when, by total coincidence, he comes here next week. I thought the official would be pleased to hear this news, but instead she scowls and says sarcastically,

"We'll see. Come back next week and we'll see." What a horrible experience. Why does she dislike me so much? In the middle of the night the answer suddenly comes to me. Mrs Nasty doesn't want to issue my identity card as she believes Croatia is only for Croatians! As far as she is concerned, I wasn't born in Croatia, therefore I am not Croatian.

The following week I return to the police station. The birth certificate has arrived and once more I am at the mercy of Mrs Nasty. Her attitude hasn't improved and she sneers as she looks over the document. Painstakingly slowly, she looks through all my documents again before picking up the telephone to call the police officer in the office across from her to ask him about me and my application. Quite blatantly she suggests to him that she should not approve my application! But, what she doesn't know is that he is one of our neighbours in Račišće. She becomes angry very quickly when he tells her that there is absolutely no reason why she should not grant it. With a particularly sour mouth, she completes the paperwork and tells me to come back in three weeks to pick up my card.

Well, I am so glad that's over and done with and I certainly won't be going back to see her again if I can help it. So much for my idea of relaxing and eliminating stress.

Later that day, I'm in the kitchen cooking when there is a knock on the door. I'm not expecting anyone and I can't imagine who it could be. Two men and a nervous woman are standing on the doorstep and in broken English the woman explains she was born and grew up in our house. She is wondering if she can have a look through the house to see what we have done to it. She's anxiously biting her lip when she walks into our bedroom.

"This is the room I was born in," she says before promptly bursting into tears and sobbing uncontrollably. It seems that whatever emotions these people show they do so with excess. Within a matter of days a younger woman from Korčula also appears. She, too, was born in our house and she doesn't get beyond the kitchen before she breaks down!

Having uplifted my identity card from Mrs Nasty I am now entitled to a concession on the ferry to and from Korčula island and I am also eligible to vote in the election here. There is a political meeting being held in the village hotel tonight and I am keen to go. If I am voting then I'd like to check out the candidates.

It is pouring with rain as we leave for the hotel, I'm late arriving and the meeting is in full swing as I enter the room full of people, but there is not another woman in sight. The meeting is somewhat quiet with no debate, let alone any heated debate and it takes me only a few minutes to realise why. There is in fact only one party present – HDZ. Political views are strong in this village and often dictate friendships. It would probably be virtually impossible to have a multi- party meeting here as many of these people are just far too volatile and they would be at each other's throats. I recall one day not very long ago, when Denis and I were talking to friends on the waterfront, who were, by the way, members of the HDZ party, we waved to someone we knew, as he drove past and the man we were talking to, responded with,

"Him! Bloody communist!"

From a political point of view, the village is divided in two. On the east side, the residents consider themselves conservative right wingers whereas, on the west, they consider themselves socialist or communist. Living here on daily basis it is quite common to hear either side refer to the other as fascist or communist. On one occasion someone actually suggested to Denis that he was a fascist because he was wearing a black shirt!

We have encountered many older people here and also a surprising number of younger ones who still bemoan the current government and the loss of communism.

Witnessing this political behaviour would undoubtedly have disturbed my father. He would have been angry listening to the stalwart communists and their constant comments about how they wish that Tito was still their leader. My father had an abhorrence of Tito and believed that he was nothing more than a skilful, charismatic trickster who duped his people for his own ends.

Regardless of the odd turnout at the political meeting, I exercise my right to vote and I am surprised to see that my name is actually on the electoral roll. The village voting results come through and the vote is split fifty/fifty between the HDZ (democratic union or centre right) and the SDP (left wing labour or socialist party, formed out of the rebirth of the old communist party). HDZ declared independence in 1991, precipitating the beginning of the war.

It's hard to believe the time has gone by so quickly and surprisingly it is now September, my favourite time of year here. Summer is on the wane, the sting has gone from the sun and it's cooler at night for sleeping. The arrival of autumn also brings our possessions by sea to Zagreb, which is great, but the associated paperwork is not. We have hired a customs agent in Zagreb, but apparently we are compelled to use the local agent in Blato as the shipment must be cleared in the area, in which we live. This is the beginning of a very protracted saga. Having filled in a clearance application this must now be notarised. There is a notary in Korčula, but she is closed for six weeks holiday and the only other notary is in Blato. As we don't have a car, Ranko very kindly offers to take us there.

The notary's office is in one of the narrow, cobbled, back streets. From the outside it is nothing special. It just looks like the rest of the ancient, stone houses adjoining it.

It is just past six o'clock when I arrive and already there are about twenty people waiting, milling about and chatting on the doorstep.

At precisely six-thirty an old, battered, yellow car pulls up. A grey-haired man gets out of the driver's seat and proceeds to unpack a vast quantity of files and books from the boot.

Unkempt, straggly hair covers his face and impedes his vision as he struggles to close the boot of the car. In the end, juggling the load under his arms, he succeeds.

A woman gets out of the front passenger seat in a particularly leisurely way. She too has grey hair and it's long, unwashed and greasy. She is overweight and has an ample bottom. The brown trousers encasing it look so tight I wonder if the seat seam will split. She ignores the man with the cumbersome load of books as she puts her brown bag on her arm and struts towards the office door. The sea of people opens for her. *She* must be '*The Notary*'. There is further commotion as the man attempts to unlock the office door without dropping his burden. Despite the fact that she does nothing to help him, once again he succeeds. He must have done this many times before, but the look of severe irritation on his face tells me he is not enjoying it. They both enter and he slams the door in the face of '*would be*' clients who resume chatting. Presumably, this must be a regular occurrence.

Five minutes later, the door to the waiting room opens and the wave of people, which has now become even larger, surges inside. The ten seats lining the walls are taken by the elderly and the excess continue to mill about restlessly. I begin to wonder how they will determine who goes first and what order they will be in. As there is no receptionist, I can only wait and see.

The door to the inner sanctum opens to admit the first client and enables me to have a brief, peek inside. The floor is bright, green, artificial grass! Drab landscape pictures adorn the back wall and there are two desks, one at each end of the rectangular shaped room. A photocopier sits between the desks. The man's books are now stacked in an orderly fashion on what must be *his* desk. '*The Notary*' is admiring herself in a mirror on the wall as she runs a comb through her hair.

Time is ticking by as each client seems to take too long. I doubt that all the people who are waiting will succeed in attending to their business tonight. Miraculously, everyone knows their order. No one tries to go in out of turn, but I cannot stop my rising frustration as they all take so long. Are they chatting or do they all have lengthy paperwork for notarisation?

Loud orchestral music erupts from the pores of the office. I imagine it's to drown out the voices and keep secret the nature of the business going on within.

At twenty minutes before eight it's my turn. The male assistant closes the door with a loud crash as I sit down. He looks extremely harassed and his face is shiny with sweat.

The notary sits calmly behind her desk; straight-backed with her hands together on her blotter, she resembles a cruel queen on a throne.

I sign the register, but it then becomes obvious that I don't speak enough Croatian for us to proceed further. In an exasperated tone he fires several questions at me which I cannot understand and rifles through my papers so roughly I fear he will rip them. Unfortunately, it also becomes apparent that he speaks very little English.

Without warning he stands up, throws his arms in the air in a gesture of frustration, and pulls open the door to the waiting room.

"Does anyone speak English?" He shouts in a loud voice.

"I do!" Answers a slight, well-dressed, middle-aged man.

"Come here!" Orders the notary's assistant pointing rudely at the man.

"You are from New Zealand? You must know my cousin Peter Poša, the guitarist." The newcomer says, addressing me casually. The assistant is becoming more and more agitated as he tries to enlist the newcomer's help; however, the newcomer won't be put off. If he's going to translate, then I must answer his questions first! I look across at the notary and she is leafing through her receipt book. Adding up the day's takings on her calculator! Obviously she does not help with paperwork, no matter how busy her assistant is.

Fifteen minutes later, the assistant hands the notary my papers and she signs them hastily. Her fat fingers are drumming loudly on her blotter, I believe she is done for the night and wants to be on her way. As I thrust my papers back into their envelope, suddenly with her cold, money-hungry eyes fixed on me, she shouts,

"You must pay now, in cash!"

With her greedy, fat fingers, she snatches my money and begins to count it ravenously.

It is not yet eight o'clock as I linger in the waiting area to finish putting my papers away in their envelope. The notary is urging her assistant to pack up. It's time to go. Take the money and run, it seems. Leaving him to contend with his books, she rushes past me heading for the door. The people who have not been able to see her stare at her open-mouthed and dismayed. An elderly man moves towards her, a look of anger and dissatisfaction covers his wrinkled face as he glares at her fiercely.

I am now ready to meet with the local customs agent and as he will be in Korčula tomorrow I have arranged to meet him there at the customs office. He's late and when he eventually arrives he gives my papers a disinterested, brief glance. I know from the agent in Zagreb that I am classed as a returning citizen and therefore I am exempt from paying duty or tax. This careless, local agent offers to clear my goods early if I pay him a percentage of tax in cash! I am horrified and adamantly refuse. His response is to shrug his shoulders and tell me he's running late for another appointment. What about my clearance, I want to know? With another shrug he says he will file my papers with customs in Dubrovnik. I don't like or trust him. He has a bad aura about him and he won't look me in the eye. It is now the beginning of October, we're leaving for New Zealand at the end of November and my personal effects need to be cleared before then as I will be away for four months. A couple of days later, the customs agent in Zagreb advises me that they cannot keep my goods in Zagreb any longer and they will be delivering them to my house, but as they have not yet been cleared, a customs officer will accompany the delivery and seal the area containing the goods. Fifty-five boxes containing our possessions are duly stacked in the empty bedroom downstairs; the door is closed and sealed with brown tape and the official customs stamp.

Time is moving on and I have heard nothing from the agent in Blato. I have tried ringing him several times, but as soon as he realises it's me, he hangs up. The agent in Zagreb has also called him and he assures her that he has filed my papers with customs. I can do nothing but wait. One afternoon, several weeks later, while we are enjoying lunch on the terrace, I hear footsteps coming up the steps beside our house. Visible over the edge of the terrace is a man badly in need of a haircut. His big, ugly afro makes his body look too small for his head and for a minute I don't recognise him, but when I do I can't believe my eyes; it's the customs agent from Blato. What could he want? Perhaps he has my clearance. No, of course he doesn't. He wants more ID from me! My passport and identity card are insufficient and he also wants to be paid seventy kuna to file my papers with customs in Dubrovnik! His stay is brief and he is gone as soon as he has copies of my driver's licences and his money. I'm now completely disgusted with him and feel like kicking him down the stairs!

Over another glass of wine and the remainder of our lunch, Denis and I decide we have had enough. The customs agent is absolutely pathetic. We were told he had filed the clearance application months ago when obviously he had done nothing of the sort. This last bit of bad behaviour is the straw that breaks the camel's back. Together, we prize the seal off the door and slit open the bottom of the boxes which have items in them that we need to take on our short trip back to New Zealand. Once we have everything we need, we reseal the boxes and re-stick the seal on the door. As I predicted, the clearance does not come through until a month after our arrival in New Zealand.

Recipes

Salata od Hobotnice (Ranko's Octopus Salad)

1 kg octopus
2 bay leaves
juice of 1 lemon
2 cloves of garlic
chopped parsley
2 tbsp olive oil
2 tbsp red wine vinegar
salt & pepper
cherry tomatoes
cooked diced potatoes

Place washed, cleaned octopus in a large pan with enough water to cover it. Add bay leaves. Cook over medium heat for 1 ½–2 hours until tender. Drain well. When cool, cut into small pieces and place in a large bowl. Add the remaining ingredients and season to taste with salt and pepper.

12
Visitors

One of our neighbours refers to the path behind our house as *'Flower Street'* and in May and June each year it is a profusion of self-seeded, wild, bright red poppies. I love to wander and enjoy the lush garden we have created here and watch the poppies waving in the light breeze. Bees love it here too, especially in June when my lavender plants are ablaze with their beautiful, purple flowers. Lingering on the path, surrounded by flowers, I stop to soak up the view towards the sea. The mountains on the mainland in the distance are very clear today. Their dark, silver grey contours sit majestically on top of the ever blue sea. Soon the first of our visitors will arrive and I can't wait to show off *'Flower Street'* and also the wonderful view towards the mainland from the top of the path.

Keith is an experienced traveller and Croatia must be one of the few places he has not been. Our first visitor, he is only with us for a week, but he manages, quite successfully, to turn parts of our house upside down especially when he seems to forget that his belongings belong in his bedroom and not in the kitchen! One morning, Keith becomes entranced with the local fish vendor who arrives early every morning in summer selling fresh fish from his little, blue truck. Keith buys a particular local fish that we never buy because we don't like it and just to ensure we are put off it forever, at the end of our meal Keith puts the fish heads in the charcoal embers of our grill fire. The stink is absolutely dreadful!

Keith does provide good entertainment though. It seems he went all the way to Russia before coming to Croatia, to meet a lady friend called Vinka. Being newly single I think he had hopes for him and Vinka, but that was before he found out about Vladimir – Vinka's other half!

As an archaeologist, Keith is impressed with the stone walls and terraces in and around the village, but saddened to see that many of them are breaking down and destined to disintegrate completely. We offer him a wall at the back of our house which is in need of repair, but disappointingly he declines!

Next on our list of visitors is my brother, Colin, an airbrush artist who lives at Waipu in Northland, New Zealand. Colin will be hoping to take photos of the superb landscape here, particularly the rugged, mountainous mainland, which is usually clearly visible from here and also the island of Hvar, which often appears shrouded in mist and beautiful, hazy, muted colours. This will be his first visit to Croatia and on the day he and his wife arrive, the weather is grey and threatening to rain. They will only be staying for four days and unfortunately the weather gets worse with leaden skies and persistent rain. We are all kept inside by the weather for the duration of their visit. However, it's not all bad as it gives us an excuse to eat and drink! There are still plenty of summer vegetables in our garden and I prepare tasty meals. I'm particularly pleased with my salad, which consists of rocket, figs, pršut, and pecorino cheese with a lemon, honey and olive oil dressing. It's a fabulous combination.

The weather could not possibly have been worse than it has been during the last few days. Colin has had to settle for some dim shots taken in the drizzle and photos of Ranko's daughter who is very photogenic with her father's bright blue eyes and clear olive skin. Colin also paints portraits so at least he won't leave empty-handed.

Unbelievably, an hour after Colin and his wife leave, the rain vanishes and the sky clears to a brilliant blue. He must return another time to take the photos he missed out on.

The arrival of hot weather brings our next visitors, my daughter Rebecca and her partner Marcel. They are en route to London having left Thailand and Cambodia where they have been sweltering in Asian humidity. They will spend two months with us enjoying the sun, sea, food, and wine before job hunting in London. Every day the sky is a never-ending blue and as the days pass it becomes another long, hot summer. By now, we are all suffering in the heat and have begun to slow down. Work has come to a standstill and it's far too hot for any of those insane activities like cycling or tennis. We'll leave that to the red-faced tourists who don't appear to have noticed the heat and are continuing to indulge regardless. Most of our days are spent swimming, eating, reading and sleeping. There is plenty of time for cooking and our lunches, which have a huge selection of vegetables and often don't include meat, are long and relaxed and often followed by a siesta. Everyone becomes addicted to my tomato flamiche, my far breton made with figs and also my Croatian pepper biscuits. The only cloud on the horizon is Rebecca's tooth.

The dentist in the hospital complex in Korčula arranges an x-ray, which costs the equivalent of $10NZ, which shows she needs a root canal. It will be necessary for her to visit the dentist once a week for the next six weeks. The total cost will be about $300NZ; substantially cheaper than in New Zealand where it would cost at least $800. The dentist, a slight, dark-haired, young man is both confident and competent. His assistant, a horsey blonde in a short, tight, blue uniform is quite peculiar. In fact, I'm not quite sure what her actual job description is, as other than flirting with him, while she sits on the window sill swinging her leg, chewing gum and folding small, white towels, she doesn't noticeably do anything else. He gets no help with his instruments and her computer skills appear to be sadly lacking. Her only duty seems to be answering the telephone. Her lazy, laid-back behaviour makes the whole experience somewhat bizarre.

I sit and wait for Rebecca in the dentist's waiting room, surrounded by patients with decaying, rotten, unsightly teeth. There are very strange superstitions here surrounding teeth, which may well contribute to the poor dental care that seems to be prevalent. I'm told that many women won't have a tooth extracted when they have their period as they believe they will bleed to death! Neither do they go swimming at this time of the month for the very same reason! As to what excuse the men have for not addressing their dental hygiene, I've yet to find out.

Not long after Rebecca's visit to the dentist, both Denis and I discover we need to go there also. I have broken a tooth while biting on an overly crusty sandwich one day in Blato. The day I get it repaired, though I try to pay, the dentist insists on repairing my tooth for nothing. He says his payment is the other patients in my family that I've brought him. We began to believe he is brilliant, nothing like the rip-off dentists in New Zealand and Australia. However, unfortunately the wonderful service doesn't last. By the time Denis goes to see him for two fillings and a clean, his boss, the owner of the dental practice, has returned from leave and her equipment is constantly malfunctioning. To make matters worse, although Denis arrives on time for his appointments, she is either late or not there! She cancels several of his appointments and it is weeks before she finally finishes the work he needs doing. On his last visit, when he tries to make an appointment for me to have my teeth cleaned, she says,

'No!' The machine that has been out of action for three months is still not working! The initial speedy service had been too good to be true, but at least it is much cheaper than the dental prices in New Zealand or Australia.

I ended up seeking out the services of a private dentist who was recommended to us by our auto mechanic! I was most impressed when I arrived for my appointment with his sparkling, new surgery and his array of expensive equipment, but I had no idea what I was about to go through. He installed me in his fancy chair and absolutely smothered me with towels. I was trussed up as if I was in a strait-jacket and it didn't occur to me to wonder why. Five minutes later, despite the towels, my entire face, neck and body were soaking. Not only did I get my teeth cleaned; I got a complete water bath! Completely oblivious to my sodden state, all he said was,

"Why do you want your teeth cleaned? Croatians don't have their teeth cleaned! I hate cleaning teeth!"

After more than two months of chilling out and with deep chocolate suntans it's time for Rebecca and Marcel to leave. We bid them goodbye at Dubrovnik airport as they catch the plane to London to re-join the real world of nine-to-five jobs in the big city. We are sad to see them go, but we know it won't be long before more holidaymakers are on our door step.

We meet John and Frith from New Zealand, who are here for a month's holiday and staying in one of the neighbouring houses when John comes looking for Denis hoping he'll fix their broken shower tap. John is half Croatian and half Maori and Frith is part Filipino. Together, they look like the golden couple with their dark tans and exotic good looks. John is extremely humorous and not long after we meet them we can't help laughing when he explains the two sides of his face to us. His left side, which looks perfectly normal, is the Croatian side and his right side, where there is a huge gap as one of his teeth is missing; is the Maori side! All four of us get along extremely well and while Frith and I talk books and reading, John is off to the olive grove to grub weeds with Denis in an attempt to reduce the spare tyre he says he's developing around his middle.

The house they are staying in belongs to the parents of one of his Croatian friends from New Zealand. Frith and John were under the impression that the invitation for them to stay was rent free, however, one afternoon when Denis and John are enjoying a beer together in our courtyard an old woman appears and does a double-take when she sees John. Straightaway, she begins shouting loudly at him in Croatian. For some unknown reason she appears very angry with him. We have seen her and her sister around the village and we refer to them as grumpy and greedy, she, for obvious reasons is grumpy! On this particular occasion she has taken it upon herself to bellow at John and tell him he must pay rent. The house they are staying in is not actually her house or her family's house as far as we know and it seems very strange that she should decide to interfere in something that does not appear to be any of her business.

We learn later that many of the locals believe all people who live in Australia or New Zealand are wealthy and accordingly when they come to Račišće, they should pay plenty! We are still choking on that particular statement when another resident tells us that as foreigners we will never be accepted here even if my ancestors were born here! Prejudice runs deep in this village with many of the locals openly stating their dislike of 'Jews, Arabs and Blacks'. Their excuse being that they don't want Croatia to become like France, Spain and Holland with their migrant mix of population. I can't help but wonder if this is a hangover from German, Austro/Hungarian, and Italian Fascism.

A few days later, things come to a head when Ivan's parents arrive and ask John and Frith to first pay rent and then leave! The invitation they had from their son seems to be null and void. The atmosphere is too frosty for John and Frith and they depart quickly to stay with relatives further north in Croatia and a week after their departure the entire house is refitted with new expensive windows and doors!

So far we have had several visitors to our new home in paradise and we hope for many more. We love entertaining and treating people to traditional, Croatian food and local wine. We've had only one complaint from our guests; they didn't stay long enough to fully appreciate and enjoy the beautiful island that is Korčula.

Recipes

Zucchini Fritters (Pohane Tikvice)

4 large zucchini
2 eggs
4 tbsp flour
sunflower oil for shallow frying
salt and pepper
chopped parsley
grated parmesan cheese

Peel and grate zucchini and place in colander. Sprinkle with salt and leave 30 minutes to 1 hour. Drain and remove excess moisture by squeezing them. Place zucchini in a bowl with flour, eggs, salt and pepper and mix well. Shallow fry in oil until golden brown. Sprinkle with parsley and cheese.

<u>Roasted Peppers (Pečene Paparike)</u>

6 red elongated peppers (this variety is best as they are much sweeter)
2 tbsp olive oil
1 tbsp balsamic vinegar
2 cloves of garlic

Preheat oven to 180°C. Cut peppers in half lengthwise and place on baking paper in a baking dish. Sprinkle with crushed garlic, balsamic vinegar, olive oil and salt. Roast the peppers for 30 minutes until they are soft and beginning to char.

Flamiche (Pizza Blanche)

The Dough
1 level tsp dried yeast
300 gm white flour
1 level dessertspoon salt
sufficient water to mix dough to a bread-like consistency

Topping
1 tbsp olive oil
200 gm sliced red onions
cocktail tomatoes to cover the surface of the flamiche
3 eggs
300 gm sour cream or crème fraîche
salt pepper and nutmeg to taste
Gruyère or other cheese to sprinkle on top

Put flour, salt and yeast into a large bowl and combine. Add the water and mix until everything comes together to a stiff consistency ready for kneading. Knead for about 8–10 minutes and form into a ball. Place in floured bowl and cover with a tea towel and leave in a warm place to rest for 1 hour.

Flour baking tray and turn the dough on it. Flatten the dough into a circle to fit the tray making a ridge around the edge to contain the filling.

To make the topping, heat oil in small frying pan and sauté onion until soft. Cool.

Mix together eggs, sour cream and halved tomatoes. Add onion and mix together. Season with salt, pepper and nutmeg. Spread onto dough and scatter with grated cheese.

Bake for 15–20 minutes until golden brown. Cool on wire rack.

Croatian Pepper Biscuits (Paprenjaci)

750 gm plain flour
250gm butter, cut into small pieces
200 gm sugar
200 gm ground walnuts
2 eggs
2 egg yolks
3 tbsp honey
1 tsp nutmeg
1 tsp cinnamon
1 tsp ground cloves
1 tsp white pepper
2 egg yolks for brushing
walnut halves to decorate

Preheat oven to 200°C. Sift flour into large mixing bowl. Add butter and rub into the mixture. Add the rest of the ingredients and mix to a smooth dough. Chill in the fridge for 30 minutes. On a floured surface roll the dough out to 7–8mm thickness. Cut into shapes and transfer to baking sheet. Brush with egg yolk and decorate with walnut halves.

Bake for 15 minutes and cool on wire rack.

Far Breton

This is actually a specialty of Brittany where they bake it with prunes but I have adapted it using figs.

400gm poached strained figs
50gm rum or preferred alcohol
50gm melted butter for greasing
130 gm sugar
220gm eggs or 4 large eggs
110gm plain white flour
pinch of salt
750gm cold full cream milk

Soak figs in alcohol for a few hours or overnight if possible. Preheat oven to 200 °C. Brush 20 × 25cm dish with melted butter. Mix the sugar and eggs together and add the flour gradually, then the salt. Whisk in the milk to make a thin batter. Spoon the figs into the buttered dish and warm in the oven for a few minutes. Remove from the oven and pour in the batter.

Bake for 10 minutes and then reduce the heat to 180 °C for a further 25–30 minutes. To check if the far breton is cooked, dip the blade of a sharp knife into cold water and pierce the centre. If the knife comes out clean, it is cooked.

13
Acquisitions

So far, we have resisted having a landline telephone and television here, but we have decided that without them we are becoming too isolated. The telephone is cheap. In fact, the day I call to apply for a new line, there is a special running. The new line costs one kuna or 25 NZ cents! Max TV and ADSL broadband have just become available in our village and although it takes me longer than it should to organise, they too are both good value; however, my biggest problem, turns out to be obtaining the modem. The delivery contractor for Max TV is in the habit of delivering the modems to a café in the village. As there are no streets here, only house numbers, it is much easier to deliver them here for collection by whoever has bought one. Weeks go by and my modem still does not seem to have arrived even though I have rung the delivery man several times and he is certain he has delivered it. I soon realise that the café owner is running a side-line business selling modems that are not collected. He simply tells you your modem hasn't arrived and when you give up asking for it, he sells it! Small-time corruption is common here, and this is the second time I have encountered it, the first being the customs agent. Finally, after insisting to the café owner that he has it, I get my modem. It transpires that this is the third one that has been dispatched to me! Needless to say we don't drink or eat at that particular café any more.

As we now have a telephone and a television it seems the time has come to consider buying a car. As much as we love our island existence sometimes we find it just too inconvenient to rely on bus transport. But, as we have no garage it would be pointless buying a new car as it would only deteriorate outside in the weather. Although we've been looking, so far, we have not yet come across any suitable cars. They are either brand new, or far too old, rusty and unreliable.

We've given up searching for the time being when unexpectedly, we come upon the perfect car. An old VW Golf for €1,000. Its previous owner, a very peculiar woman, is returning to New Zealand after her unfortunate husband took his own life recently in the downstairs of their home. The woman was not well-liked in the village and sadly some people have commented that she drove her husband to his untimely death. For us, the car is a good buy having had only one owner and spent its life in a garage. Denis not only cleans, polishes, and repairs it; he ties a bunch of herbs onto the rear view mirror to chase away any evil spirits the previous owner may have left behind! It's great having our own wheels; so much better than having to put up with the bus timetable, which was always inconvenient.

With the renovation of our house virtually complete; that is, if the work on an old house is ever finished, Denis is looking for a new project. When word reaches the village grapevine that he wants a new interest, we acquire three groves of olive trees from an elderly man with the same surname as me. Ante, now lives in Germany for most of the year and he gives his trees to us to care for, as he is too old to work them. There are twenty trees in total in different areas. We are extremely excited by this impending new project and set off with Ante to inspect the groves. Very quickly, we realise he hasn't been to any of the groves for several years when he has terrible trouble finding them in the maze of ancient stone walls which are totally overgrown with dense scrub. We hack our way in and just in case we are not able to find the trees again, we mark the track with red and white tape.

The first grove in the area of Vrvala has by far the healthiest trees and the least amount of weed and scrub that needs to be cleared in the immediate vicinity of the trees.

In Glava, the trees are badly neglected and one looks as if it's almost dead. We are standing on an ancient, stone wall surveying the grove, when a pheasant suddenly emits its unmistakable call. I'm convinced that it's my father voicing his approval of our new olive tree project.

The third olive grove is in Ždrilo on the way to the neighbouring village of Kneže and it takes us some time to find these trees. The pathway is very overgrown and several times we lose our way as we take wrong turns. Although this grove is the most neglected and overgrown of all, we know that the trees here will soon recover once we begin to care for them. This site, on an elevated terrace, is probably the best of the three groves with all day sun.

In and around this village there are approximately thirty to forty thousand olive trees, which were planted during the last three hundred years. Today, less than 10% of these majestic trees are maintained and harvested. The huge remainder are completely ignored. Factors such as the declining population in combination with lack of interest and foresight and general laziness have all contributed to the state of the trees. Other villages such as Čara, Pupnat and Blato have thriving agricultural industries and co-operatives from highly productive vineyards and olive groves. What does the future hold for this village? Will the population continue to decline? Will the next generation realise the value of their land and all that it is capable of producing and begin to work it again and start their own co-operative?

My father tamed his farmland from one hundred and fifty hectares of scrub, bush and noxious weeds into highly productive, dairy land. He toiled seven days a week, as did his father before him. I remember so well my father's permanently cracked, red-raw hands. I know that he would be extremely disappointed to see the land here reverting to wild neglect. I am glad he is not here to see all this land reduced to such a sorry state.

Although she still kept contact with family in her homeland, my grandmother constantly instilled in my father that it was time to forget the motherland and focus on a fulfilling life with new opportunities in New Zealand. I believe this is part of the reason why my father never had an overwhelming desire to return to Croatia until late in his life and of course by then, it was too late.

After their twenty years or more of neglect, our newly acquired olive trees will need extensive pruning, regular fertilising and time-consuming clearing of a particularly nasty creeper with a barbed hook that has invaded many of them. Getting them into shape is a hard task, but Denis takes it on with enthusiasm and before very long they begin to respond well. We feel an incredible sense of self-satisfaction knowing we have done all the work on these trees ourselves and achieved such a wonderful result. This November, they will produce a small crop for us to harvest. If we are lucky maybe it could be as much as one hundred kilos and by the end of next year, by which time they will have had a huge amount of intensive care, they should yield a much better crop. Even though we know our first harvest will be small we cannot help but look forward to the first pressing of our own olive oil. It really is a dream that we never thought we'd be able to fulfil.

14
Finishing Touches

"I can't start work without some rakija!" Says Karlo before downing two glasses in rapid succession.

The village idiot and his assistant have turned up at our house! We will never forget Karlo and Lazar arriving to install our new, timber, exterior doors. The doors have been made by a local craftsman in Blato who is a friend of Karlo and Lazar's. Lazar, has been hammering, crashing and swearing haphazardly for only a short time when he decides to take a break from removing the old, rotten doors. Stumbling down the stairs, he arrives at our kitchen door and says,

"Here, have some grass. I have plenty good stuff!" His slurred voice is directed at Denis and I or anyone within ear shot, including a couple of friends who have just arrived to visit. Clearly Lazar is already as high as a kite on his *'grass'* and it's probably no wonder it takes him some time to complete what is actually a difficult job. As work progresses slowly, Lazar's language deteriorates; his voice gets louder and becomes more and more obscene and surprisingly it's in English! Karlo stands by and does nothing other than offer ineffectual words of advice, which only seem to enrage Lazar even more. They are both so strange we can't quite believe it and neither, I'm sure, can our neighbours.

The time has come to renovate the last major room in our house, the bathroom. We have had a good respite from the hammering, crashing and mess that alterations bring and as it's summer the pygmy bath must go! It's the smallest, weirdest-shaped bath I've ever seen and we have both had enough of trying to squash into it. The weather in August is still hot and we can use the outside shower while Ranko rips the existing bathroom apart. Once he gets started it looks worse than a bomb site. Everything must go. The fifty-year-old pipes smell and are breaking down and it will only be a matter of time before one of them bursts. He must replace all of them including the waste pipes. The new plumbing shop in Blato supplies and delivers everything we need from the tiles to the toilet; the job gets off to a good start. After a lot of deliberation we have also decided to move and replace the toilet and hand basin in the konoba. At the moment the toilet is right by the door, in a very public place. It needs to be moved to the back of the konoba and a bamboo screen erected in front of it for privacy.

The entire job should be relatively simple; however, when Ranko's father-in-law arrives to do the plumbing, he turns out to be a pompous, grumpy, pain in the neck. We have strife with him as soon as he begins working. He looks at our new pedestal hand basin and says it's too small and we should take it back. Little do we realise that this is just the beginning of his list of complaints. It seems that our new bath is also too small, the toilet can't go where we want it and neither can the bath taps! He doesn't seem to consider that the room is quite small and would look absurd the way he wants it. After a heated argument with Denis, which Mr Grumpy tries to conduct in German, we get our own way. But, it doesn't stop there and very soon the plumber is shouting yet again at Denis.

"Guma! Guma!" He insists. Neither of us have any idea what he is talking about. As far as we know, '*guma*' is a tyre. What on earth does a plumber want with a tyre? Thinking he has made a mistake, Denis ignores him. But, the grumpy plumber persists and repeats his request in an even grumpier voice. I too am baffled until Ranko explains that '*guma*' also means hose!

As the job moves on, obviously the plumber appears to be annoyed that we didn't take his advice and I'm sure just to irritate us, he insists on putting up the towel rails. This time he comes up against me as he argues about where they should go and I won't budge. His response is to sulk and take forever to put them up. In the future, if we need a plumber we sure hope that there is another one available! Despite the grief given to us by the bossy plumber, three weeks later our new bathroom is a lovely luxury. Ranko has done his usual perfect job for a very good price; however, he looks more than a little embarrassed when he gives us the plumber's invoice. We are sure he knows that it is higher than it should be and there is more. The plumber wants to be paid immediately! We know that the plumber is grumpy and we have also heard that he can be greedy too and now that we have received his invoice we know that this is also true. We're certain the plumber is not poor as we've been told he spent a number of years working in a foreign country where he earned good money. He was one of the privileged few who were permitted by Tito to work in a abroad. We have always wondered why he received special privileges, until recently we learned that his uncle, who was one of Tito's secret police, arranged it for him.

Ranko, Denis and I are sitting under the walkway outside the kitchen in the cool of the evening enjoying a glass of wine and a bowl of our own marinated olives. They are so good it's difficult to stop eating them. Having finally exhausted the discussion about the new bathroom and the plumbing, our conversation turns to water and our cisterna. We are connected to the town water supply now and do not use the water in our cisterna. Denis wants to drain it and stop it being refilled, but Ranko believes we should empty it, clean it out and let it fill again during the winter. In fact, he is quite empathic when he says,

"You never know when you might need it and you must have it ready in case you do." As I've said previously, Ranko tends to talk only when he has something important to say and with that in mind, after a brief discussion, we decide to take his advice.

What an unpleasant job it is to both empty the cisterna and clean it. We siphon the water out with the garden hose and let it run under one of the lemon trees. It smells so putrid we are concerned that one of our neighbours will smell it and complain. Fortunately, we're lucky and they don't appear to even notice what we are doing. In order to scrub it out, Denis has to use our ancient, blue, timber ladder and climb inside. I can't face it. Just looking inside it makes me feel claustrophobic. Then, I start to become stupidly nervous when the cat goes right to the edge to investigate the hole where the cover has been removed. I take her away as I'm sure she'll fall in. After several days of Denis' hard work the cisterna is clean and now all we need is rain to refill it.

By February the cisterna is almost full and it is just in time as something has happened to the village water supply and it has stopped. For three days the village is without water, but we are fine as we have switched over to the supply from our cisterna. Unbelievably, only a few days later the town water dries up again and this time it's even worse. There is no water for five days and a water tanker arrives to supply the houses that normally rely on town water.

Looking through the junk in our attic, wondering what useful things may still be hidden there, Denis uncovers the original, interior, window shutters. In many of the houses here the original windows and shutters have been replaced with new plastic-coated, aluminium ones, but for us, these do not fit in with the old, traditional look we are hoping to achieve for our house. We have no idea why the original shutters have been removed as there doesn't appear to be anything wrong with them. On one side they have been hand carved with a simple stylish pattern and all they need is sanding and repainting. They're good, solid timber and as we're quite taken with them, we have decided to restore them and put them back at the same time as we repaint the window frames. The result is amazing. It's a superb touch that not only looks great but also keeps out the light and the cold at night. As we enjoy a glass of wine and admire the finishing touches that have just been added to our house I wonder if I will ever want to leave this place. So much of my being is here now and we have put so much effort into restoring and nurturing our house. It feels as if, finally, my soul has come to rest.

15
Fruit of the Land

Living in Račišće permanently, we begin to measure the year not by the days as they pass, but by the seasonal harvest from the rich, fertile soil and the produce from our own organic garden. As the seasons change, we are continuously offered new delights; wild blackberries in July; figs in August; grapes in September; almonds, walnuts and pomegranates in October; wild strawberries and olives in November. To add to our organic garden, Denis has brought a tamarillo, a feijoa and a lime tree from New Zealand. I was doubtful that he'd manage to get them into Croatia until he came up with this very novel idea. By putting flowers around them, he turned them into a giant, floral arrangement! As we passed through various airports on our way to Croatia several officials asked what he was carrying and when he replied,

"Flowers for my grandmother!" They waved him on through.

Miraculously, the plants survived the journey and the following season the tamarillo produced thirteen fruit. It was with some hesitation that we brought the tamarillo tree here as we were concerned that it might not be suited to the climate and die during its first cold winter while we were away in New Zealand. Luckily, the tree is fine even though there was a light dusting of snow in the village during winter and it looks as if it will bear even more fruit this coming season.

With the fantastic selection of produce here, we eat like locals now. Our main meal is in the middle of the day, mostly on the terrace when it's fine, but when it becomes too hot, in order to escape the heat, we move our kitchen dining table outside under the shade of the walkway adjacent to the kitchen. It's far too hot here, in the height of summer to consider eating upstairs on the terrace, even underneath the umbrella. Almost every meal during summer is tasty and varied. Our organic garden provides us with an abundance of tomatoes, zucchini, rocket, eggplant and beans.

The ground was infertile and unproductive when we planted our first vegetables and flowers, but now, thanks to three years of compost and olive crushings, the soil in the gardens surrounding our house is vastly improved. Here, it is traditional for women to tend domestic gardens and men are seldom seen working them. There have been numerous occasions when Denis has been digging in the main vegetable patch beside our terrace, when men walking down the path have seen him and they cannot keep their mouths shut.

"What you doing? That women's work!" They shout, shaking their heads. They also seem to think that as he digs the vegetable garden then he must also plant the flowers, even though they only see me working in my flower garden! We both laugh when they compliment him on his beautiful flowers.

During the four to five months of the summer season there is usually little or no rain and it is necessary to water our gardens daily. Luckily, we are able to use the water supply in our cisterna. Not only is it convenient, but it also saves us paying to use the town water supply. The heat in August is intense with temperatures often in the mid-thirties. Some plants simply cannot survive and die. During the cold, wet winter the only plants that survive in the vegetable garden are kupus, garlic, onions, silverbeet and broad beans.

In Račišće, there is one particular fruit of the land that deserves special mention and that's mushrooms. The mere thought of the mushrooms that appear each year in November sends our friend Pavo into a spin.

"You haven't seen anything like our Croatian mushrooms," he says just about every time we see him, in the weeks leading up to the mushroom season. Pavo has learnt from his father, who in turn learnt from his father, where all the different mushrooms grow. Unsurprisingly, the spots have become a heavily guarded, family secret. There are about thirty different varieties of mushrooms that grow here, predominantly under olive trees. We've been told that there are two varieties that are poisonous, but nobody seems to be able tell us which ones they actually are and when Denis tells Pavo he's been asking people about them Pavo tells him off.

"You must not talk about mushrooms. What I tell you about them you must keep to yourself. It is a secret for your family and mine only!" He says, putting his finger to his lips.

The mushroom varieties pop up in cycles and as one variety finishes another one starts. Pavo's favourite mushroom, which he describes as the blue and red one, pops up first. We are rather repelled by his description of it, certain it must be a toadstool and we can't wait to see what it really looks like. It's early morning when we set out to search for Pavo's special treat.

"Where are we going? Is it near those blackberries I showed you a few months ago?" Denis asks Pavo as we trudge off into the unknown.

"Blackberries? Did you pick those?" Pavo replies obviously avoiding any comment on where the special spot is.

"Yes, I picked them. They were growing on the side of the road."

"They might be, but someone will still be 'master' of those blackberries. You must ask permission!"

"But, they were growing on the side of the road," says Denis.

"They may be, but someone will still be the 'master' of them and you must ask, otherwise there could be problems."

"OK," says Denis, bemused. "But, where are the mushrooms?"

"Easy boy, easy! Soon you will see. The hills have ears so we must be quiet and if any cars come we must hide quickly. Anywhere! We must not be seen!" For a short time I wasn't sure what Pavo meant when he said that the hills have ears, but then it came to me. It is a hangover from when the country was under Tito's leadership and the control of his secret police. They have been gone for more than thirty years now, but I guess old habits are hard to break.

Intent on his purpose, Pavo begins to walk faster when suddenly a car approaches and he indicates that the three of us should dive into the nearest ditch or blackberry bush as it turns out! Not long after we come out of hiding we reach the special spot, but unfortunately there is not a mushroom in sight.

"Doesn't look like there's any here Pavo," Denis says with great disappointment.

"Patience. I will show you. There's plenty," Pavo replies, smiling. What is he seeing that we cannot?

"Wait. I must go first," he says, holding us back with his hand. As we watch he walks slowly and deliberately towards something invisible. Carefully, in the mounds of leaf mulch, he begins to dig with his hands and unexpectedly there they are, plenty of mushrooms hiding under the decaying mulch. We hasten forward and are vastly relieved to see that in reality they are actually a copper oxide colour on top. Maybe Pavo is colour blind!?

Laden with two bags of mushrooms, we are on our way home when Pavo misses his footing and he dislodges a rock from an ancient, partially collapsed, stone wall. We can do nothing but watch in silent horror as his round, overweight body falls, head first as if he's belly flopping into the sea. It's funny, but we are unable to laugh. For a start, we've been told to keep quiet in case someone sees us in one of the special spots and secondly, he's fallen quite a distance, which isn't very funny as he could be seriously hurt. When he rights himself his hat has been knocked from his head and we are surprised to see that he is bald, but as he is never without his hat, we had no idea. There is a gash above his right eye; his lip is bleeding, as are both his hands. Strangely, he is not concerned about his injuries and all that bothers him is that someone outside his family might discover this mushroom spot.

"If anyone asks you about my cuts say nothing. Don't tell them anything at all. Don't even tell my wife. Not even she is trustworthy. She's never learnt about the mushroom places," he says, rubbing his head with his sleeve to wipe away the blood. This wasn't the first occasion Pavo had made derogatory comments about his wife. I recalled the day she planted parsley seeds far too thickly and his comment was,

"I know one shouldn't say bad things about one's wife, but my wife, she is not dumb, just stupid! I am only telling the truth!" Then there was the time she dyed her dark brown hair very blonde and I said to Pavo,

"Your wife's hair looks great doesn't it?"

He responded with, "Hair look it good, but still same old brain!"

On the journey home there are no cars to be seen, which is just as well as we can't imagine diving into the bushes with our mushrooms or the injured Pavo. The following day, outside the store, all Pavo's mates rib him about his black eye.

"What you been up to? Did you fall down?" They joke and laugh as they admire his swollen, discoloured eye.

"No!" Says Denis, stepping in to help Pavo out,

"His wife punched him!" Pavo seems happy with this as; at least they haven't suggested he injured himself while mushrooming!

Back in the kitchen the blue and red mushroom with its truffle-like, leathery texture is tough and we consider its best use to be in a stew or a casserole.

The next mushroom that appears is shaped like a large chalice and has red speckles on top of it. There are several varieties in this family, but the locals will only eat the one with the red speckles. We thought that maybe some of these ones could be poisonous so we asked Pavo, but he did not know.

Next, in the selection is a light-coloured one that looks like a frilly skirt. This variety tastes best grilled. We are in mushroom heaven when the dome-shaped black and white champignons appear. There are lots of them and their flavour is magnificent. Jozo, Pavo's son, picks one the size of a dinner plate and much to our surprise, he gives it to us. Unbelievably, the locals don't like this variety and don't eat them. From this giant we cook a huge pot of soup, which is absolutely delicious.

Mushrooming here is very competitive and many of our expeditions take place at odd times. One of the best times to pick them, according to Pavo, is on Sunday morning when half of the village are at church! By the time the bumper season has finished, although we are all mushroomed out, we are very happy with our freezer full of champignons.

My favourite fruit from the land is without question figs. Here, there are three types of figs; a small green one, a large green one and a black one with the best flavour and the firmest skin, which doesn't fall apart during cooking. As the locals do, we, too, dry plenty of figs in the strong summer sun and with our abundance of basil I make spiced fig and basil jam. This year I came across a new recipe for glazed figs using lemon slices, cinnamon quills and cloves. Unable to contain my desire to sample them, we opened the first jar just two weeks after I made the first batch and much to my delight it was delicious.

Word has got around the village that I make jam and now when the figs are ripe, locals turn up on my doorstep with figs, jars and sugar. I don't know if they have forgotten how to make it or whether they never knew, but they are very grateful when I give them back their jars filled with jam.

As the land provides us with an abundance of fruit so, too, does the sea. Of course, fish has always been one of the main sources of food here and for many of the locals this is still the case. The small boats moored in the bay come and go all year round and most of the locals are very keen fishermen.

In summer and autumn there are squid, octopus, sardines, anchovies, eels, mackerel or lokarda as they are called here and also a red fish called trilja or kopači. Lokarda, we don't enjoy; it's very dry and gives off a rather unpleasant smell when it is being cooked. The red fish we avoid whenever possible as it is riddled with small bones. In fact, we have yet to understand why the locals like it so much; we find it very fleshless and nothing but a mouthful of bones. Crabs can be caught all year round and crab baskets are popular. Denis found the granddaddy of all crabs living in a small cave on the waterfront. It seems that lots of people know about him and although many have tried to catch him, he is too smart and so far no one has succeeded.

My favourite fish are the fresh anchovies. We eat them often for lunch, tossed in wholemeal flour and lightly fried in our own olive oil. Not only are they delicious, they are extremely cheap.

Every summer, Denis and Pavo prepare ten kilos of salted fish for eating during winter. They buy fresh sardines or anchovies from the fish truck that comes to the village each morning. Denis cuts off the heads and guts the sardines while Pavo packs them into tins layered with five kilos of sea salt. One kilo is left whole and ungutted. This tin is especially for Pavo's father who prefers to eat them whole in the traditional manner. Once the tins are full, they are sealed with a lid with a rock on top, and left outside in the sun for two months. At the end of this time, the liquid is drained off and the tin refilled with brine. On the first occasion when Denis helps Pavo with the salt fish there is a bit of confusion as to the strength of the brine. Denis is all set to weigh out the salt quantity, but Pavo stops him.

"Weighing the salt is not necessary. All you need is a potato!" We couldn't imagine what he meant, but he was insistent. We had no choice but to watch and wait. Firstly, Pavo adds salt to the water in the bucket and stirs the brine. Next, he drops in the potato.

"You must watch the potato. If he swims, then the brine is the right strength!" He says. It's without a doubt the funniest recipe for brine I have heard of; however, it appears to work. Once the tins are refilled with brine and resealed in the same manner as before, they must be stored inside the konoba, where it is cool, for four to six months. After this time the sardines may be eaten immediately or removed from the tin, washed, repacked in olive oil and stored in the refrigerator. Denis loves them, but they are an acquired taste and altogether too strong for me.

Never before have I seen such as an abundance of fruit produced by such fertile land. As the seasons change and the choice offered, changes with them, I don't believe I will ever grow tired of this lush, green paradise.

Recipes

Glazed Figs

1 kg ripe figs
2 lemons
700 gm sugar
1.5 cups of water
3 tbsp ground ginger or 50 gm whole ginger
1 tsp whole cloves
2 cinnamon sticks

Trim the stems on the figs and cut a small cross on the base of each one. Slice the lemons thinly. Simmer the figs, lemons and spices in the water and spices for 5 minutes, add the sugar gradually and simmer over a low heat until the figs have become glassy and the syrup is thick, approximately one hour. Bottle in sterilised jars immediately.

Spiced Fig and Basil Jam

1 kg ripe figs
500 gm sugar
1 tsp cinnamon
half tsp ground cloves
zest and juice of 1 lemon
bunch of roughly chopped basil
3 cups of water

Cook stalked and chopped figs and water over low heat until soft. Add sugar and stir until dissolved. Add the rest of the ingredients and bring to the boil. Boil until thick and sticky. Test on saucer from freezer and bottle in sterilised jars when skin forms on jam.

16
Harvest Season

The village olive press is expected to open on the first of November. It did not operate last year as it was closed down by the council for illegally discharging waste into the sea. Apparently one of the residents in the village contacted the Ministry of the Environment and made a complaint about its operation. Apart from damaging the sea's ecosystem it also caused several of the waterfront properties to turn green.

Our friend Clare, who lives on the village waterfront, was most upset about the pollution and took a sample of sea water.

We were back in Noosa during this time and she posted the sample to me to be analysed. She packed it in a small perfume-like bottle and marked it 'Eau de Račišće!' I was astounded that the sample actually made it through the postal system, however, it did and I took it to the Ministry of Health for analysis straightaway. The results showed an extremely high copper content and also a high bacteria count. Unfortunately, these results were not able to be used as evidence in Croatia, but it didn't matter as by this time, the authorities had already closed the press.

We've been told that the owner of the press has recently spent some time installing a sump for the waste, so the problem should not occur again this year.

The press here is a relatively new Italian, traditional, cold press. Last year, when it was closed, the olives from Račišće were taken to the press in the neighbouring village of Kneže. This is a centrifugal press and the general consensus seemed to be that it is not as good. Some people complained last year that their oil was bitter and blamed the Kneže press. The *'experts'* in the village seem to hold the view that the bitterness comes from a combination of two elements – the type of press and the lack of rainfall. Without sufficient water the olives ripen too quickly and their low moisture content causes them to produce bitter compounds.

At last, the day has arrived when we will harvest our first crop of olives. Picking our small crop takes only a week, but we are pleased with the harvest and believe we have about one hundred kilos to take to the press. Unfortunately, we have just been told that the press in our village will not be opening this season. We assume that the owner has not complied with the council regulations. However, whatever the reason it seems quite peculiar having all that money tied up in expensive equipment that is not operating. We could take our olives to Blato or Lumbarda as both of these villages also have their own presses, but after meeting the friendly owner of the Kneže press we decide to take our chances there. We will find out for ourselves about the quality of their pressing.

Our booking is for ten-thirty, but when we arrive the press is not operating. There has been a delay as the truck that takes away the crushed olives, or waste, has become stuck in the mud at the dumping ground and all the workers from the press have gone to pull it out. Fortunately, the delay is short and after lunch our olives are pressed. We have one hundred and sixteen kilos, which yields twenty-seven litres of oil or 24% of the total weight. The average in our village is around 15% and apparently our percentage is the highest in the village! Within days the news of our pressing has spread and every second person we come across congratulates us. We have no idea why our percentage is so high. We do know that the olives at our grove in Vrvala were big, and very ripe and as they made up 85% of the total weight, we assume that is why we achieved our 24%. The only other reason that we can think of relates to the fact that our olives were taken to the press within a few days of being picked whereas many of the locals store their olives in barrels of sea water for weeks to save them making more than one trip to the press. As they become saturated with saltwater, these olives turn brown and we believe this must affect the quality of the oil. However, this is the tradition here and there is no way anyone can be persuaded to discontinue this practice. Whatever the reason, we are heartened by such a good result from an uncared for crop. We imagine our future crops and pressings will be even better provided that the rain and wind do not destroy the flowers before the fruit has had time to set.

It's almost time to begin harvesting grapes and Pavo is twitchy.

"I must weed my vinograd now. Harvest is only two weeks away and I don't want them saying that I'm a no good workman if they see weeds in my vinograd," Pavo says to Denis on the way to his vineyard to begin work. He is concerned that his cousin and the other people who help him pick his grapes will talk about him being lazy if his vineyard isn't tidy at harvest time. Pavo has problems with his feet and knees making it difficult for him to spend as much time as he should, tending his grapes and olives. When he and Denis arrive at the vineyard, which as always is a lush green paradise, the weeds are out of control and although some have perished during the dry summer others are still standing tall and green.

"We'll dig up the ground between the vines with the rotary hoe," Pavo insists.

"But, surely we should pull out the big weeds first," suggests Denis. "Otherwise we'll just be spreading the seeds."

"No, I always use the hoe. You will see." Pavo is insistent and his mind is totally closed to doing this any other way. Once Denis begins using the hoe, chopping up the weeds, seeds are scattered everywhere and we know that before long Pavo's small Garden of Eden will be full of bigger even more virulent weeds. Pavo, however, seems quite satisfied and is not bothered. His only concern is stopping the talk about him being a 'no good workman'.

Grape harvest is now well underway and in the evenings we have been researching various wine-making techniques on the internet. This year, we have decided to try making different wines and while he's helping Pavo and his cousin pick the last of their grapes, Denis foolishly runs our ideas past them.

"No!" Says Pavo we don't make that sort of wine here. "Why do you want to make that? It's not the tradition. You'll just waste the grapes." Both he and his cousin then laugh. They cannot even begin to entertain the idea of trying something new. We, however, are not deterred.

Using thirty kilos of mali plavac (small blue) grapes, the first wine we make is twenty litres of rosé. The grapes are hand-crushed before being put into a large bag to drip overnight into a barrel for fermentation. The following day we add yeast and leave the grapes to ferment for five days before bottling the wine in a glass vessel with an airlock. Two months later we re-bottle it into smaller bottles. We are well pleased with our rosé when we first drink it in February five months later. It's very dry with a soft, clear, pink hue and a fruity nose and even Pavo is impressed when he reluctantly tastes it.

Beaujolais is our next experiment. Using wild mali plavac grapes, this time we put sixty kilos of whole bunches of grapes into heavy-duty plastic bags without yeast. We are relying on the natural yeast in the wild unsprayed grapes. The sealed bag takes about one and a half days to expand like a balloon. Once we have pricked the bag to release the air, we leave the grapes for six to eight weeks to ferment. At the end of the fermentation we cut the corner off the bag, drain out the liquid and press the grapes in Pavo's traditional wine press. As it is in France, our Beaujolais is also very drinkable on '*Beaujolais Day*' the third Thursday in November.

If it's good enough for the locals, then it's good enough for us to make the traditional village wine using vranac grapes. An aromatic purple grape, vranac produces a much heavier wine. We have one hundred and twenty kilos of vranac, which Denis crushes in true Croatian style with his feet, which become stained dark red. Once the yeast is added, this wine has a very quick fermentation, which lasts only three to four days. The wine is full of sediment and it is necessary to rack it at least four times until it becomes clear. We taste it, and it is ok, but we know it has room for improvement. We believe the grapes we bought were probably picked too early and their brix percentage was not high enough. There is a tendency here to pick grapes and olives, for that matter, before they are fully ripe. The locals simply add sugar to increase the brix (sugar concentration) to 20%. We don't use sugar and once again we are laughed at, but at least our wine is very drinkable, unlike the sugary, purple death we sampled at the pompous, grumpy plumber's house!

Having had good success with the wines we have made so far this season, now, we become even more adventurous and decide to make some prošec or late harvest wine using wild, black grapes that we picked late in the season. After ten days of drying in the sun, the brix shoots up to 29.5%. We crush them in Pavo's press before leaving them to ferment without yeast or sugar for a minimum of three months. Nine months later as I write this I'm drinking a small glass of our prošec and eating trapist, aged, cheddar cheese from the island of Pag. Prošec has a nose similar to sherry, but the flavour is more like a ruby port and I'm thoroughly enjoying it with the cheese.

Near the end of his wine-making, Pavo calls Denis for help with his second batch. He's already made one thousand litres of wine and now he is making a further two hundred litres using the strained crushings from his first fermentation to which he has added extra sugar and water. This time the fermentation lasts longer and the result is what Pavo calls his second class wine for his own consumption, whereas the first batch, he will sell. He's called Denis to help him with the filtering process. Instead of using a normal filter he jams a prickly plant, which is a cross between wild asparagus and gorse into the drain hole of the barrel. It's a very spiky plant and gloves are essential to handle it. Denis first came upon this plant some months ago when he was helping Pavo clean weeds from underneath his olive trees. When Denis tried to remove the plant, Pavo insisted that he leave it saying he would need it for filtering his wine. At the time we couldn't imagine what he intended to do with it, but today it's all been revealed and it works very well.

Shortly, as we have finished our wine-making, we will have a new alcoholic experience to enjoy as Pavo is suggesting we make rakija from the used grape skins. It seems like a good end use for the skins and we are keen to try it. The grape skins have been fermenting in sugar for several weeks now, while we wait for the call from Rade, who owns the village still, to tell us when he will make our rakija.

The copper still is thirty years old and was set up by Rade's father. Every village on the island is allowed to have one still provided the rakija is for domestic consumption only. Payment for Rade's services is by way of cash or goods such as wine or dried herbs or Rade will keep a percentage of the rakija.

Rade phones to say that he will be making our rakija tomorrow morning. He will light the fire under the still at four-thirty am and we will need to be there by six-thirty am bringing with us some small, fast-burning, fire wood. The still needs about two hours to reach the right temperature and once we arrive the process will begin.

At six-thirty it's still dark when Rade begins issuing instructions to Denis. He must chop wood, sterilise parts of the still between batches and tip out the skins at the end.

Rade sits by the ferociously hot still monitoring the process constantly, and after an hour, when the first drops of alcohol emerge, I know I am experiencing something quite unique.

The still is located outside Račišće on the way to the neighbouring village of Kneže on Rade's little farm. Here, where the soil is rich and fertile, there are well-tended, olive trees and grape vines separated by ancient, stone walls. Nestled amongst the trees, close to the road, are Rade's rusty old sheds. Goats and pigs snort and snuffle in the nearby enclosure as the big old still which is charred black, burns fiercely.

Already, Rade's mother is working; every morning, she is up early tending the vegetable plot. Today, she is weeding the tomato patch which has stinging nettles growing in it. She is not wearing gloves and I am astounded to see her grab the giant nettles by their leafy stems and simply pull them out. Never before have I seen anyone uproot such a vicious weed with such bravery. If it has stung her then it's not obvious as she tosses it in the rubbish with apparent ease.

Back at the still, Rade's face is bright red as he feeds wood onto the fire and steam curls out from under the lid. Rade is huge. Well over six feet tall, he has giant proportions. His appearance itself is enough to make you laugh, but it's actually his voice that is the most humorous. It's incredibly tiny, high up and squeaky.

The distillation process goes without a hitch and it's obvious that Rade, having learnt this particular skill from his father, knows exactly what he is doing. Our skins yield five litres of rakija, which we are looking forward to tasting in a couple of days.

Pressing our olives and making wine are our two favourite seasonal highlights. Our olive oil is superb and we believe with its beautiful, rich colour and spicy flavour it's the best we have ever tasted. After loads of research and only two seasons of practice our wine making is progressing well and we know that already it surpasses many of the locals' wines even though making wine has been their family tradition for more than two hundred years.

17
Village Life

For a number of the women in this village, their lot in life is gruelling. Many of the men here are seamen and spend months at a time on board ship. Our neighbour's husband has been away now for five months and in his absence she just has too much to do with only the help of her aged, frail mother-in-law and her teenage son. She has just finished making three hundred litres of wine when she collapses from exhaustion and spends several days in bed. Today, however, her smile is back. Her husband will be home in a few days, in time for the olive harvest. Hopefully, once he returns it will be sometime before I see her, as I often do, with a heavy-duty line trimmer strapped to her body or wielding a chainsaw to cut up firewood.

Unfortunately, her break is short lived when her husband has a turn and ends up in hospital with heart problems. A heavy smoker, as many of the people here are, as cigarettes are far too cheap, he needs an operation and is not able to do any physical labour for some time. We hope not only that he will recover, but that he will seriously consider giving up smoking otherwise we fear he will meet his end sooner than he should.

When it comes to health issues here many locals choose to ignore them. It's not that the health system is inadequate or that the waiting list for operations is long. Perhaps they just hope that their particular problem will go away if they pretend it doesn't exist or maybe they believe that they can cure it themselves. Whatever their reasons, I am about to experience the health system as I must go to Dubrovnik hospital for a small operation.

"No. Not on your side. Get on all fours and put your behind in the air! " The large authoritative nurse with the penetrating eyes orders the patient in the bed next to me. Screens around beds don't exist here. I can't watch and I turn away and bury my head in my book. I really don't want to see what unmentionable thing the poor woman is having done to her now. All morning she has looked as if she is in severe pain. Her operation was scheduled for earlier in the day, but they must be running late.

It's dinnertime and I've had no food, just water for two days as my operation isn't scheduled until tomorrow. I hope they bring me something to eat, even if it's light; maybe some thin soup perhaps.

Here comes the pretty, blonde nurse in her blue uniform bearing my dinner in a small, metal bowl covered with a lid. Yuk! Sweet, warm, red-coloured, metallic-tasting liquid! It's perfectly horrible. The bowl is only about a third full and I don't even know what it is I am drinking!

Here comes a doctor on his rounds swaggering in the door, his mouth exaggerating the chewing of his gum. His swagger is so extreme he almost looks as if he has a limp. He is a George Clooney lookalike and very much in love with himself. His harem of blue-uniformed nurses stick to him like a stamp on an envelope, hoping for an even better view of his hairy chest or more likely what's beyond it as his white uniform is already unbuttoned to his navel! Perhaps, if I were twenty years younger I would be lusting after him too. He is cute and has captivating sparkly eyes.

It's the middle of the night. A noise has woken me up. There it is again. Crinkle, crinkle, crinkle! The Slovenian woman across the room is sitting up in bed. The noise seems to be coming from her. But, what is it? I gaze around the room. This wing of the hospital is fairly new. Subdued lighting high above our beds casts a faint glow on the pale, yellow walls, but all I can make out is a vague upright outline of her and I can't see what she might be doing. Silently, she gets up and as she walks past my bed to go to the window, she uses the foot of my bed as a handrail. My bed shakes. Crash, bang, slam! And as if that's not enough, the noise she makes opening the window in the middle of the night is deafening. Having finished tampering with the window, she returns to her bed, but not before letting go a sulphuric fart. She tends to do this several times a day and I have begun covering my nose with the sheet each time she heads my way!

My operation has been and gone. Thankfully, it was a simple one and now I'm allowed three meals a day, but every time my food arrives, I feel like I am in a Russian labour camp. All that's missing is the cold! Bread and cream cheese for breakfast and of course my favourite red tea. Lunch is dishwater soup with a few specks of rice plus more rice and a small piece of grey meat. Dinner is more bread – dried out and left over from breakfast I think and more dishwater soup with the odd carrot floating in it. Everything in a metal bowl has, of course, that special metallic flavour!

In the middle of the night, the crinkling noise wakes me again; however, I know now what it is. Mrs Slovenian's husband brings her eight or nine different chocolate bars each day at visiting time. She devours them all in one go, in the middle of the night. When morning comes, if you happen to be looking, you will see her stuffing the empty wrappers in the bin before the nurses see them. You may wonder if she is fat. The answer is yes. Very!

As I am awake now, and hungry, I eat the banana that my husband brought me earlier in the day. Unthinkingly, I leave the skin on top of my bedside table. When the big, bossy nurse with the severe eyes comes to make my bed at five-thirty the following morning she picks up the banana skin and roasts me for eating it! I can't tell her how awful the food is and how starving I am so I stay silent. She scares me!

I am happy with my surgeon (not George Clooney). He is very professional. My discomfort is minor and my scars will be minimal. I appear to be the only one of the three in my room to get personal attention. Today, he has visited me three times! He too is a good-looking man apart from his typically Croatian flat head! I have noticed Mrs Slovenia looking him over and today she accosts him as he is leaving the room.

"It's my leg," she says rubbing it. "Can you come and look at it? It hurts all the time." Her operation by the way was abdominal. Clearly, he has no time for her and dismisses her coldly as he says,

"You have already been here for ten days and it's high time you began to walk around and get some exercise. Nothing else will help your leg and besides I am not your doctor!"

Her mouth turns down at the corners and she goes into an immediate sulk. During the three days that I have been here, she has limped around clutching chair backs and bed heads. But now, all of a sudden, she comes to life, rips open the wardrobe doors, strips off the clothes she's wearing and throws them onto the bed as she puts a backless, halter dress onto her naked body. I try to avert my eyes. I forgot to mention that not only is she fat, she is at least sixty! Without as much as a backward glance she runs out the door as if she is being pursued by an angry swarm of nurses. She is gone for three hours. I have no idea where she could be.

Mrs Slovenia's husband is visiting today, as he does every day. He seems a gentle, patient, smiling man. Short, grey haired and fit-looking, he opens his back pack. First out are the chocolate bars. She smiles and has trouble taking her eyes off them as he puts them into the drawer of her bedside cabinet. Today, he has more presents for her. There is a large bag full of new clothes with the tags still attached. She spends a long time looking through them, whining as she goes. Occasionally, she tries on one of the garments ensuring that her husband knows she really doesn't want to. Her mouth has regained its sour expression as she shakes her head and stuffs all the clothes back in the shopping bag before telling her better half to take them away. The poor man. I feel sorry for him. With a shrug and a fixed smile on his patient face, he pecks her on the cheek and leaves. She ignores him and sits unhappily on the bed with her legs crossed, staring at the wall in a trance.

It's time for the doctor's rounds as Mrs Slovenia strips off her t-shirt. The fried eggs on her chest sag and she is naked except for a small pair of purple knickers pushed too low by her rotund stomach.

'George Clooney' walks in, blue eyes flashing. No gum today. Mrs Slovenia is in the first bed as you enter the room and he stops at the foot of her bed.

"My! My!" He laughs. Her face lights up as she pulls her shoulders back and tries in vain to achieve the pert breasts she might have had when she was sixteen (but I doubt it). From across the room George catches my eye. I can see he thinks she is a joke. She bats her eyes at him and he manages to turn his smirk into a candid smile before he moves on.

Every night it's the same. Crinkle, crinkle, slam crash. I feel so tired after my broken sleep and still there is another hour to go before breakfast. Perhaps I can go back to sleep. The patient in the middle bed looks as if she is asleep, but Mrs Slovenia is up. She must be in the toilet. My thoughts are confirmed when firstly, I hear the machine gun sound of her farting, and then the room fills with a foul, clogging stench. Covering my head with the holey sheet, I imagine what I'd like to say to my doctor today, if I had the courage.

"Please, can I go home? The patient in the end bed is in the wrong hospital!"

'Herb' women are still found here and many people believe that herbs or 'trava' as they are called here, can cure almost anything. Pavo often wraps his feet in silverbeet to cure an ailment that we cannot quite determine. Perhaps he has gout, arthritis or maybe even something worse such as a verruca or an ingrown wart. I did suggest that he cut down his excessive consumption of red wine and meat, but he wouldn't hear of it.

Just yesterday one of the old people in the village died and today cars are pulling up outside the church for the funeral. There are no parking spaces left by the time the owner of a newish-looking VW Golf arrives so he decides to double-park. We are standing chatting to Ranko on his balcony when the VW slowly begins to make its way across the road. The owner has forgotten to put on the handbrake, but he has locked the car. It all happens so quickly that there is nothing anyone can do as the car picks up momentum and nose dives into the sea.

Yet another death means I will attend my first funeral here. On Saturday the policeman's father, who was elderly and had been sick for quite some time, died.

The cemetery looks particularly beautiful as the chrysanthemums from All Saints Day are still blooming brightly. The tiny chapel, where the coffin is resting, is open and seats have been arranged for the immediate family. As the village people arrive the formality of this Catholic funeral becomes evident. Both the men and the women are in dark suits and most of the men are wearing black ties. The immediate family and the priest are amongst the last to arrive. Marijan's widow looks extremely upset and sad. She is actually wailing and crying out in Croatian as she enters the chapel holding her son's hand. It is the local custom for the congregation to go into the chapel and greet the family and as Denis and I file in and I embrace the widow, her wailing, which had ceased, suddenly begins again in English and I become aware that this is solely for my benefit.

"My Marijan's gone and he's never coming back," she calls out in a stricken, anguished tone. It's too much for me and I break down along with her two youngest grandchildren. I have always seen her as a strong woman, but today, she appears very fragile dressed all in black including her head scarf which is tied under her chin.

Next, the priest recites prayers with only the family inside the chapel before the coffin begins its final walk around the perimeter of the cemetery. A group of women carrying wreaths lead the procession and the coffin, pushed by six men, follows.

Walking beside the family, behind the coffin, is the priest, followed in turn by the rest of the congregation. After the small circuit is completed, to the accompaniment of the church bell, rung by one of the village elders, the procession comes to a halt at the graveside. The priest once again recites prayers as he stands next to the lone altar boy dressed in purple and white robes and holding burning incense. Only the immediate family are clustered next to the open grave. At the end of the prayers, the lid is removed from the coffin exposing the body, which has been wrapped in a special way, inside a sheet. Marijan was a very tall man and I am horrified when I see his feet wearing blue socks, protruding from the sheet. It is very harrowing and no doubt these people are used to it, but I certainly am not. Coffins are not common here hence the communal coffin which is kept in the chapel. As our friend Ranko is very strong he is often asked to lift the sheet-wrapped body into the grave. Once the body is in the grave, the marble cover is then rolled back over the grave. Finally, for those who wish to attend, there is a mass held in the main church back in the village.

As one person passes away so another is born. Our neighbour Sanda has given birth to a cute baby boy who has been named Ivan Botica. This particular name is probably the most common name in the village and he will be about the thirtieth male here to be given this name. For obvious reasons it will be necessary to address him by his family nickname.

Together with the people who inhabit Račišće there is also a large population of cats. For some reason, I'm not altogether sure whether it's cost or in fact superstition, it is not the fashion to take your cat to the vet to be de-sexed. Consequently, the cats here breed like rabbits, that is except for our cat 'Noosa' who we have decided must be sterile as even though she comes into season regularly and receives vast amounts of attention from the surrounding males, she never gets pregnant. When I mention this to a neighbour another funny superstition surfaces when the neighbour says that it's impossible for our cat to become pregnant as she has two homes!

We have come to dread the times when our cat is on heat. Firstly, there is the howling of males at night, which keeps us awake, and secondly, it seems to me as if our cat turns into an absolute tart when she brings home the mangiest, dirtiest males that we didn't even know existed. All of them know how to be persistent as well as pee on the doorstep, that is, if they're not actually already having sex with Noosa on our doorstep! We have taken to spraying them with the hose and we keep piles of rocks in strategic places to pelt them. One of the worst intruders was a ginger tom and no matter what we did to him, short of killing him, we couldn't get rid of him. He'd sit gazing at Noosa with his soppy, love-struck expression as he edged closer and closer. We'd bombard him with rocks and chase him away only to find that two minutes later he'd circle around and reappear on the other side of the house, while during the whole performance Noosa rolled over and over, shamelessly flirting with him until he got too close to her when she'd whack him on the nose with her claws!

Just when we thought we were finally getting used to the marauding male cats, pregnant females and the endless litters of kittens that always seem to be around, dogs suddenly started to appear. If the locals are not prepared to de-sex their cats then they are hardly likely to de-sex their dogs. Whenever the grubby, apricot poodle at Noosa's old house finds a female on heat, it barks constantly day and night and the rest of the village dog population joins in. Strangely, the locals seem oblivious to it. We can't sleep and we wonder how they do. Maybe they have earplugs or perhaps they're deaf or they simply turn up the volumes on their televisions! Like the cats, it's inevitable that any female dogs will get pregnant and needless to say they do and sometimes to the most unsuitable breed. An example of this is the dog that I call '*the cat gone wrong.*' If I didn't know better I'd swear that one of its parents was actually a cat.

Recently there's been an increase in the number of small ankle-biting dogs and one of the worst offenders is the postman's dog. Fortunately, it doesn't live at the post office as if it did, I think someone, maybe even Denis, would have done it in by now. If you walk past the postman's house and the dog is not tied up then he circles around behind you barking ferociously and even though he looks like a harmless dirty, small, white, puff ball, he does his best to bite your ankle! I don't know why, but the postman thinks it's funny. Obviously, he has a warped sense of humour. I am not amused and I don't think the postman will be either if and when the day comes that I'm forced to use the stick I now take with me whenever I walk past his house, which I do on most afternoons as it's on the way to Vaja, my favourite beach.

As well as being entertained by the village animals there is also a varied selection of amusing local characters hanging about outside the store, drinking beer in either the early morning or the evenings. It goes without saying that there are never any women in this group as men and women do not socialise together in public here. On the rare occasions when you actually see a man walking with his wife, she is usually the compulsory three paces behind him!

Amongst the cartoon characters there are, '*Big Nose*' who has one of the reddest, ugliest, bulbous noses I've ever seen. He is a diehard communist who loves to lecture anyone within earshot on how bad the country is now that it's no longer ruled by communists; '*Short Pants*' who always wears ripped off jeans in the summer as he is under the mistaken impression that his legs are worth looking at; '*Earring*' who has a huge blockhead and is more often than not, drunk; *'I'm the Most Handsome Man in the Village'* has given himself his nickname believing that even with his seriously undershot jaw and pot belly he's God's gift to women; '*Yellow Hair*' who is well over sixty, uses peroxide on his grey hair in an attempt to turn it blond hoping his new, much younger, girlfriend from Herzegovina will find him more attractive; '*Broad Bean*' is absolutely addicted to broad beans and if he had his way he would eat nothing else. He is somewhere around seventy and enjoys telling anyone who will listen that his wife, who is fifteen years older than him, no longer gives him his conjugal rights and he's had to resort to watching blue movies on television late at night!

Sometimes, in the hotel, if you strike it right you will come upon the village's six, most famous bachelors. None of them have married and they were all in the same class at school. Now, as they are over sixty, I imagine there is almost no chance that any of them will find a wife. This is such a peculiar coincidence I can't help wondering if there is some root cause. Was there something in the water they drank or are they all 'gay'? Apparently there are no 'gay' people in this homophobic village or if there are, they have either moved away or, for obvious reasons, hidden their sexual persuasion.

Village life here is refreshingly different. Some aspects of it remind me of New Zealand in the 1960s when I grew up in a rural environment and to some degree this is appealing. Children amuse themselves with simple games without their parents having to entertain them or buy them expensive toys or computers. We are learning to live with the unruly population of dogs and cats, but the one thing that we cannot accept is the total disregard for keeping the environment healthy. The habits, which the locals indulge in, illustrate their abuse of the environment quite clearly and they really are quite appalling.

When your car is old and sick and about to die, you just drive it up the back somewhere behind the village and abandon it permanently. It then becomes a prime target for vandals who invariably smash it up and remove the tyres rendering it a total eyesore destined to remain there forever. It's the same fate for old appliances. There are many dumped on the walkways behind the village. The nearest tip is in the village of Lumbarda which is not far, but it seems that people here are just too lazy to take their rubbish there and prefer to tip it over the side of the nearest bank. Slowly, but surely this village is being defiled by inorganic rubbish. We have voiced our opinion on the subject to several of the locals; however, they show no interest, simply shrug and walk away. We have also endeavoured to clean up the concrete area around the store, which is littered with rubbish, by placing a rubbish bin there. But, every morning when Denis goes to change the bin liner, it is gone and the rubbish bin is tipped onto its side so it that can't be used. After a few days we discover that Andrija, the store owner, is the culprit and when Denis confronts him, he says he doesn't want a bin outside his shop as all it will do is attract rubbish! The conversation between him and Denis gets so heated that it turns into a shouting match and they end up not speaking to each other.

A few days ago, we witnessed what may be a glimmer of hope to solve this problem, when the 'Green Lady' from Zagreb visited our village to present Clare, our Australian friend, with an award for keeping the beach on the waterfront in front of her house, spotlessly clean and tidy. We can but hope that the locals will take note and begin to change their ways.

18
More Rules and Regulations

Denis has become an overstayer! His visitor's permit has expired and as we are now living here permanently, he must apply for a temporary stay permit and also citizenship on the basis that he is married to a Croatian citizen. We had hoped that our lawyer in Dubrovnik would have been able to file both of these applications and although he tried, unfortunately the authorities knocked him back. It seems that the rules have recently changed and now these applications must be filed in the country of one's birth.

At the end of November, we are returning to New Zealand where we will spend four months in Auckland escaping the European winter and also hopefully sorting out Denis' permit.

The day following our arrival in Auckland we visit the Croatian consul in Henderson and file both applications. The consul is quick and efficient and all that remains now, is for us to wait as absurdly both applications must be sent to Zagreb before they are then forwarded on to the police station in Korčula.

Two months have gone by and despite the consul contacting Zagreb several times, we have heard nothing. We will be returning to Croatia in early April and if Denis hasn't been granted a permit by then, we are concerned that they will not allow him re-entry. At the beginning of February we finally have a response. Our expensive, certified, translated, apostilled marriage certificate has been rejected. It is one day too old! It was valid when we filed the application with the consul, but as they took so long to look at the application in Korčula, they have now decided it is out of date and we must produce another one. It takes us some time and a considerable amount of money to obtain a new one and when the consul sends it, she also reminds them of our impending arrival in Croatia. Their only response is to ask for more papers, including a letter from me giving Denis permission to live in our house! As time moves on, we are becoming increasingly anxious about Denis' permit especially with these very strange paperwork requests.

The permit has not been granted and we will leave without it. There is nothing else we can do. During our stopovers in Paris and London with Rebecca and Marcel we are determined not to let the inefficiency of the Croatian Internal Affairs Department spoil our enjoyment of these two wonderful cities.

On the day of our arrival in London an unexpected email arrives from the Croatian consul in Auckland. Denis' permit has finally been approved and the Croatian Embassy in London will issue it. We celebrate with a night out at Guy Ritchie's pub 'The Punchbowl' in Mayfair. The young, Irish chef is a friend of Rebecca's and we are treated to a fabulous meal.

Winter weather in both Paris and London has been cold and as we fly out of London we wonder what we will find upon our return home to Croatia. Apparently, it snowed, not only once but twice, in our village during our absence. As we expected it's unseasonably cold when we arrive in Dubrovnik. Much to our severe irritation, because of Easter, absolutely everything is closed here. It's unbelievable. We even have difficulty finding a meal and to make matters worse, we have no choice but to stay a couple of days longer as we cannot travel to Korčula until Easter is over. The usual man who takes us to the island is asking for double the fare, which we are not prepared to pay.

Despite the cold, wet winter, our house and garden are fine, even the tamarillo tree, which we were certain would have perished in the snow, is green with new spring growth.

Today, is the first day Denis can report to the Korčula police station to get the final seal of approval on his temporary stay permit as even the police station has been closed to the public over Easter. Upon our arrival there, we are greeted by an unfriendly woman who does not make us feel at all welcome.

"Let me see. Uh huh. You are one day late coming here. Why is this?" She says in a cold, stern voice.

"Am I? I wasn't aware there was a strict deadline. I mean it's Easter and as you know everything has been closed, including the police station. We've only just arrived from Dubrovnik. It was like a ghost town there. We couldn't believe that all the shops and restaurants were shut. I came here as soon as I could, you know." He replies but she is not impressed.

"Well that's no excuse. You should have presented yourself yesterday. I must consider this matter to decide whether or not to fine you for being late. Come back and see me tomorrow." The expression on her face is ever so gloating and ugly as we leave her office.

The following day she relents and is a little more pleasant as she stamps Denis' passport and orders him to present himself in her office again in a year's time for the renewal of his permit. We imagine it will be much simpler the second time around. After all we've done so much paperwork already, what more could they possibly want?

I, too, have paperwork that needs attending to. In New Zealand, I have reverted to my maiden name, and now it's time to change my name in Croatia as well. In New Zealand, the process was very simple. It took only fourteen days and required just two documents, whereas in Croatia the process is much more complicated and requires several documents, some of which are very unusual, such as documents proving that I do not owe any tax or have any debts. All going well, it should not take more than a couple of months to be completed. We have never quite seen anything like the rules and regulations here when it comes to the paperwork for permits and identity cards. We thought Australia was very strict but then we had not been here, had we?

19
New Ventures

Almost every cup of coffee we have drunk in Croatia is dreadful and we believe it's time to do something about it. I have imported a small, coffee roaster from the USA and green beans from the United Kingdom and it is our intention to roast beans in our wine cellar and sell them. As our last business was a roastery and café we have had plenty of experience in this field. The roaster has arrived by sea and with the exception of the paperwork it was not difficult to import, but when it comes to the green beans, it is an entirely different matter. We are told that we must purchase anti-corruption stamps to prove that the beans have not been smuggled into the country! I try to ring the Ministry of Finance to arrange this, but they refuse to talk to me and when I call a second time they actually hang up on me. Fortunately, my customs agent in Zagreb refers me to a second agent in Dubrovnik who is not only pleasant and helpful but speaks excellent English. Together we complete the forms and deliver them to customs in Dubrovnik. The customs officer stares at me strangely during the ensuing interview.

"Why are you importing beans? No one has ever imported green coffee beans into Split or Dubrovnik before! Do you realise that you will not be allowed to drink your own coffee?!" He comments are not only absurd, but totally unexpected.

During the lengthy interview there is a considerable amount of arguing between my agent and the customs official until finally the officer agrees to order my stamps for collection in twenty-one days. They also tell me they will mail me a return, which I must fill in once a month regarding the usage of the beans, and return to them. At the end of the interview my agent and I are so worn out we retire to a bar around the corner for a drink. He suggests I order coffee as from now on I won't be able to drink my own!

The smell issuing from the wine cellar is glorious. Freshly roasted coffee beans! Surprisingly it attracts very few of the locals. In Račišće, the locals drink predominantly Turkish coffee made from stale, inferior quality beans, which they buy in the local shop for about $NZ16 per kilo. They boil it to death and sugar it heavily to disguise the hideous taste. Given the appalling standard of the coffee here we believe that the smell alone should be sufficient to sell it. However, when Denis begins to market it, it proves very frustrating. When he talks about fresh coffee it falls on deaf ears and when he gives them samples to try, most of them complain. The beans are too dark or too light. No matter how he roasts it, they cannot be satisfied and some of them even go so far as to tell him how to roast it! We are extremely disappointed with the response. They are so resistant to change here it is unbelievable.

Feeling somewhat dejected after the coffee episode, Denis seeks refuge amongst the olive trees, pruning and chopping down some small oak trees that are blocking the light. It's drizzling when he begins and he has only been working for a short time when one of the locals pulls up in his car, gets out and comes over.

"You must not cut tree in the rain. You will make it sick!" He declares with a very serious expression on his face. Denis asks him why, but he doesn't reply. Once the visitor leaves and Denis resumes work, another car pulls up and the same conversation happens again only this time he's also told that he can't cut firewood either; it's May and wood can only be cut in August and January! We assume this has something to do with rising sap, but once again no explanation is forthcoming.

Denis' experience trying to prune the olive trees when it's drizzling reminds me of one day when we bumped into Pavo's wife.

"What are you doing?" She asked.

"Painting inside the house," I replied, whereupon she began to frown and shake her head.

"Ah no! Mokar! Mokar! You must not paint. It's no good." She then wandered off at precisely the wrong moment just as the neighbour's black cat appeared and crossed her path. She happens to be ridiculously superstitious and as soon as she saw the cat she rolled her eyes and ran! I smiled to myself at both her superstitious nature and also her use of this funny word. 'Mokar', which means soggy, damp or humid, can refer to the ground or the atmosphere. She was trying to tell me that this particular day wasn't a suitable day for painting, which was, in fact, rubbish. As it was almost summer time, the weather was actually perfect for painting! I hear this word 'mokar' so often that I have now come to realise that most of the time it is just the perfect excuse for laziness. We find it impossible not to laugh about these peculiar superstitions over a glass of wine later that evening.

With our abundance of olive oil I have decided to try my hand at soap making. After searching the internet, I've chosen an American recipe that looks fairly simple. My ingredients are filtered rainwater, lye, olive oil, lavender oil and dried lavender flowers. Much to my frustration the process is not quite as simple as I'd hoped and it takes me several batches to perfect it. One of my problems is mixing the ingredients. My soap is too runny and won't set properly. To achieve the perfect result I must beat the mixture with a 'stick mixer'. Nothing else will do. The other issue is the vessel in which the soap sets. Plastic is no good as it does not breathe. I'm really delighted when Denis crafts a special, lightweight, wooden box for me out of a tray which once contained stone fruit. It solves my problem beautifully and my soap is excellent – smooth, creamy and wonderfully perfumed with lavender. I am considering selling it in the village, but I wonder if it will prove as hard to market as the coffee beans?

There's a slightly different reaction to my soap. A handful of locals appreciate its artisan, natural qualities and the price of twenty kuna is not an issue. However, many of the villagers laugh.

"Why you make soap? It is not necessary; you can buy it in the shop, you know!" They say.

Apart from my soap the other product I'd like to sell here is bread, but alas I don't have a commercial oven. We have reached the stage now where we simply don't want to eat the bread from the shop. It has no taste; it's dry and goes stale too quickly. With the help of a Jamie Oliver recipe book and a particularly excellent book called *Crust* written by a French chef, I have begun to bake bread. I have tried my hand at several different types, including bagels and brioche, but I believe the best loaf I make is a white loaf filled with fresh rocket from our garden and Parmaleta aged Cheddar. Everyone who samples it quickly becomes addicted!

It's possible I may embark upon another new venture and consider selling my bread in the future, but for the time being I shall bake it purely for the enjoyment of family and friends.

Recipes

Olive and Rosemary Bread

2 cups white flour
1 cup wholemeal flour
1 level tsp dried yeast
1 level dessert spoon salt
1 tbsp olive oil
large handful chopped fresh rosemary leaves
15 pitted black olives
water to mix

Put flour in mixing bowl; add yeast, salt, rosemary, olives and oil. Add sufficient water and mix to a dough consistency. Turn dough onto work surface and knead for about 8 minutes until it is supple and elastic. Shape into a ball and place in lightly floured bowl. Cover with tea towel or baking cloth. Leave in warm place for one hour until it almost doubles its bulk. Remove from bowl and reshape into a loaf kneading dough to make a spine on the underside. Place on baking tray dusted with flour and leave for further hour. Pre-heat oven to 200 °C and bake for 25 minutes until golden brown. Cool on wire rack.

Focaccia with Rocket and Cheese Filling

3 cups white flour
1 level tsp dried yeast
1 dessert spoon salt
1 tbsp olive oil plus extra olive oil
1 cup grated cheese (preferably parmesan or aged cheddar)
large handful fresh washed and dried rocket leaves
chopped thyme
water to mix

Put flour, yeast, salt and olive oil in bowl. Add water and mix to dough consistency. Turn dough onto work surface and knead for about 8 minutes until it is smooth and elastic. Shape into a ball and place in lightly floured bowl. Cover with tea towel or baking cloth and leave to rise in a warm place for 1 hour. Remove from bowl and roll dough into a large rectangle. Drizzle one half with olive oil and cover with cheese and rocket. Drizzle again with olive oil. Fold lid over filled half and seal edges with thumb and first finger. Rub small quantity of oil on top of bread and sprinkle with chopped thyme. Place on lightly floured baking slide and leave in warm place to rise for a further hour. Preheat oven to 200°C. Bake 18–20 minutes until light golden brown. Cool on wire rack.

20
The Job

During the height of summer, in the months of June, July and August, it's too hot to work outside for most of the day. In the cool of the evening we wander through the vineyards and olive groves marvelling at the grapes and olives growing fat in the heat from the sun. We are enjoying our idle existence enormously until Denis gets a call from the owner of the hotel Mediteran. He wants to know if Denis will work for him, for a few days. This should be a breeze for Denis who has owned a number of restaurants in New Zealand and worked in the hospitality industry for many years.

Denis' first day starts well and although he is the only waiter working the tables it's not so busy that he can't cope. The tourists appreciate his professional service and also his espresso. Denis is an excellent barista; no one in this village can make espresso to anywhere near his standard. The tips he receives are very generous. On day two, he encounters his first problem; the toothless, feisty, red-headed Croatian dishwasher, who turns out to be the woman who helped him lift the 'dead' fridge down the steps when we were throwing out the rubbish from our house. Clearly, she knows nothing about restaurant hygiene and persists in dumping her dirty ashtrays into Denis' bar sink which is expressly for washing glasses! When he tells her not to, she does not want to listen to him and becomes hostile. Next, he catches her smoking in the kitchen while she is putting away clean plates! This time she can't cope with the telling off Denis gives her so she leaves, no doubt thinking she'll return later, when he has left for the day.

The following morning, she arrives for work in such a sulk that she won't even speak to Denis. Through the village grapevine we have heard that this abrasive, coarse woman had an illicit affair with the postman not too many years ago. At first I did not believe it as he has a very, pretty, young wife and I couldn't imagine why on earth he would be attracted to a hard, old battle-axe who already has a husband. However, I soon knew the rumour had substance when the postman came into the hotel one day and I saw the redhead giving him the eye! It's impossible not to laugh when I imagine the vicious tongue lashing she would have given him if didn't do as he was told.

Today, the owner of the restaurant is in the kitchen doing the chef's job and understandably, after working too many days and nights in a row without a break, his nerves are frayed. At lunchtime, Denis takes an order from a couple who would like to share a risotto. First, the chef becomes angry because they only want one meal and then he refuses to give them another plate and two sets of cutlery. But, the worst of it is, *he* won't relay any of this to the guests; he wants Denis to tell them! The guests at the next table order two different risottos and this time the chef tells Denis to tell them, they must have the same risotto! When Denis refuses he gets angry and shouts, "I am restoran, not café, not bank!" By the end of the day Denis is exhausted, but not from working, it's the Fawlty Towers environment and the unprofessional happenings that have worn him out.

On his last day, the locals decide to provide Denis with a challenge. Every day the hotel plays host to the card players in the village. It's not serious gambling, the main rule being that the losers of each game must pay for a round of drinks. Having watched Denis working there for a few days, some of the card players like the idea of testing him and when they arrive, even though they can see that he is busy, they shout rudely at him to get them their cards, paper and pencils from the table inside where they are kept. They are surprised, when having treated him offensively, he responds by telling them to get what they want themselves! Then they push him even further by trying to evade paying for the drinks on their tabs, but again they don't succeed as Denis is one step ahead of them. They still haven't had enough sport with him and when he comes to the table to take their drink orders, they either ignore him or speak to him in the village slang which, of course, he cannot understand. Frustrated by their attitudes and as it's his last day, he gives them back what they have dished out! Surprisingly, when the card players leave three or four men acknowledge his professionalism and compliment him with comments such as,

"You're the best waiter we've ever had. We can see that you know what you're doing!" At eight o'clock in the evening, after the departure of the card players and the tourists, Denis is still serving drinks to the few remaining lonely, old bachelors propped up at the bar when the restaurant owner turns on the television. Denis simply cannot believe the channel he chooses. It's hard core porn!

A short time later we are not surprised to hear that the hotel, which is a very, poor, tourist amenity, is for sale. Mediteranska Plovida, the company that owns the hotel and a few of the local ferries, is in dire straits. Many of the locals believe that the majority shareholder, who grew up in this village and now lives overseas, has basically ruined the company and is stripping it of its assets. A date has been set for the day of the sale and buyers are invited to turn up and pay the non-negotiable asking price of €500,000.

The hotel consists of a huge restaurant with a well-set-up kitchen and bar plus six rooms for accommodation above the restaurant. The hotel's position, right on the sea front, is superb, however, any prospective buyer will not be permitted to redevelop the site and it is also unknown what is able to be done to rectify the sewerage problem that has plagued the hotel for a number of years. In the height of summer the smell from the out-of-date waste discharge system is ripe. In earlier times, when the country was still under Communist rule, the hotel was called 'Dom za Kultura' and it was more or less used as a community centre where the village people went to watch movies, dance and play cards. Today, only the card playing remains.

Several of the locals are angry at the thought of the impending sale. They appear to feel that the hotel belongs to them, even though they do not legally own it; they believe that their effort to help build it and the fact that some of them once worked there, makes it theirs by right. They are also furious with Mediteranska Plovida as several people who used to work for the company in the hotel or on its ships have now lost their jobs. Neither do they like the idea of the majority shareholder cashing in the company's assets to feather his own nest.

Today the regulars, who invariably gather outside the store adjacent to the hotel to begin drinking beer early in the morning, are absent. The street and the waterfront are noticeably quiet. As we survey the scene a police car pulls up. It seems that sometime during the night before the sale, someone poured a ring of petrol around the perimeter of the hotel and threatened to torch it!

The day of the sale arrives and at eleven o'clock in the morning the village is invaded by men and a handful of women wearing business suits and carrying briefcases. This causes a brief spectacle as city slickers are seldom seen here. In the end, the whole thing turns into a bit of an anti-climax when no offers are forthcoming. The police remain in attendance, obviously in vain, hoping to find the culprit from the night before. Unsurprisingly, the village is still strangely quiet. It's such a small village that I'm sure more than one person knows who poured the petrol, but no one is prepared to speak up.

Months later it's summer and the hotel is still struggling along. The proprietor of the restaurant and bar is slowly falling apart. He has never worked in hospitality before and the long hours are slowly doing him in. Overweight and out-of-shape he is often slumped in a chair in the corner, when in fact he should be helping out his over-worked staff, but he seems quite content to do nothing other than berate them loudly for not providing good service. I wonder if some of the redheaded, toothless one's habits have rubbed off on him? Apparently, in the space of three months he has gone through about thirty staff members. No one can stand being abused by him and the average length of employment for each worker is about a week! It soon becomes very apparent word has got around that he is a tyrant and nobody will work for him. His last resort is to hire 'Johnny Bullshit', one of the most obnoxious characters in the village. We can't imagine 'Johnny' putting up with being abused as he is a hot-headed loudmouth. Perhaps, the proprietor will finally meet his match and 'Johnny' will give him back what he deserves!

21
Merriment in the Vinograd

What to do to celebrate Denis' birthday? The obvious choice, as it's late summer, is a grill in Pavo's vineyard.

I'm out of bed early today as the first job on my list is to bake bread. I have decided I will bake Denis' favourite, an olive and rosemary loaf.

Walking to the vineyard in Vrvala, it's hot and the sky is blue and cloudless as it has been for most of the last three months. Underneath the shade of a giant olive tree laden with partially ripe fruit, the rustic concrete table, built many years ago by Pavo's father, is set for lunch. Pavo's cousin Leko, will be the chef today, grilling pork, chicken, čevapi (small spicy Bosnian sausages), paprikas (pointed red capsicums and tikva (zucchini). I've baked a giant, chocolate cake for the birthday boy and there is also my bread, which is still cooling and promises to be splendid.

It's a great gathering that includes group of the locals, my cousin Sylvia, and her three daughters who have just arrived from New Zealand for a short stay. For some strange reason, Denis persists in calling my cousin Sylvia, Sybil, as in Fawlty Towers and I wonder if perhaps the strange happenings in the hotel have left too much of a lasting impression on him!

Leko lights the grill early using olive wood, which burns with a long intensity and produces excellent charcoal making a perfect, grill fire. Almost straightaway he begins drinking red wine in vast quantities while absent-mindedly attending to the grill. Pavo looks very amused and when I ask him what's so funny, he says that sometimes Leko drinks more than is necessary and he is thinking that today maybe, this will happen. Pavo then goes on to tell me about Leko's dubious behaviour a short time ago when Pavo gave Leko two litres of red wine. It seems that Leko polished it off before he had even left Pavo's house. By the time he staggered home, he was so drunk his wife locked him out and he had to sleep in the chicken house with the chickens! Today, Leko, who mistakenly thinks he's rather handsome with his white hair and unfashionable droopy moustache, is merely garrulous and entertains Sylvia's daughters (three attractive blondes) with slightly smutty tales from his youth.

Meanwhile, I have been talking wine and alcohol with a Croatian friend Patrick and his son who live in Perth but spend summer in our village. They have just tasted the limoncello I made using our rakija, with the chocolate cake and they would like a bottle. Unfortunately, I don't have any more as when we arrived in April this year there was not one lemon on either of our trees and as yet the crop has not replenished itself. I know the locals must have stripped both of the trees completely while we were away and when I explain this to Patrick his story is even funnier. Each time he leaves Račišće at the end of summer to return to Perth, the previous owner of his house comes from Korčula town to strip his tree. It seems that even though he sold the property to Patrick some years ago, he still thinks he owns the lemon tree. All I can offer Patrick is some rakija infused with blackberry, which I remember I made a couple of months ago. After a long lunch with both excellent food and company, we wander back to our house to try the blackberry rakija.

As the evening progresses we are joined by a group of Croatian people who live in Perth, but have returned to our village for a summer holiday. As the wine flows, the men decide it's time to sing. There's nothing like a singing Croatian male. Many of them have great voices and are not afraid to sing in public. On this occasion when Patrick, Ivo and Michel break into song, they are clearly enjoying themselves. Years ago Ivo and Michel sang together in a group and their harmonies are wonderful to listen to. After performing three songs they decide it's time to treat us to 'Konoba', a song that was written by Rujnič. Ivo tells me that this is a famous Croatian song that Rujnič wrote after he spent an evening in a konoba in Split. Apparently the barman received a phone call that evening to say that Rujnič's father had died. However, he did not know how to break the news to him, so instead he began offering him drinks. Finally, after Rujnič had had several drinks, the barman plucked up the courage to tell him the sad news. The song is about the time he spent in the konoba when there are good and bad times and people get together to drink and sing. Once the song is over it's time to call it a night.

The following day, Pavo's daughter Petrina comes to visit and return some of the cutlery we left at the Vinograd after yesterday's grill. She's looking particularly bright and cheerful and says she has news for me. About a year ago she was diagnosed with severe anaemia; she became pale and listless and lost her usual bright, sparkly demeanour. Today, she has just returned from the doctor and her latest blood test results are vastly improved. Unable to afford to buy iron tablets, she has been taking a special medicine recommended by her doctor. She insists on giving me the recipe in case I should ever need it.

First, you take two litres of red wine and add four cups of sugar, twenty, bright, shiny, steel nails; you boil the mixture slowly for two hours and once it has cooled remove the nails and store it in the fridge. Every morning for one year she has been drinking one small glass of this medicine and now it seems she is cured. Could this really have been what restored Petrina's iron levels to normal or was it the spinach she had begun to eat in large quantities?

Summer is almost gone, but as usual it's been glorious and we're so pleased to have made the most of it with enjoyable summer merriment in Pavo's vinograd.

Recipes

Limoncello

12 lemons
2 × 750 ml bottles of vodka or rakija
2 cups of water
2 cups of sugar

Remove yellow rind of lemon, taking care to scrape off any pith. Place peel in a large jar with a screw top lid and add one bottle of vodka. Place mixture in a dark place for 2 weeks. Combine water and sugar in saucepan and bring to the boil over medium heat, stirring constantly until sugar has dissolved. Cool to room temperature (this is very important-if the sugar syrup is still warm then limoncello will be cloudy). Strain the vodka from the peel using a fine sieve and mix it with the remaining bottle of vodka and the syrup. Bottle and seal tightly then store in a dark place for at least 10 days before drinking. To drink straight limoncello can be stored in the freezer.

22
The Rainy Season

The days are considerably cooler now. In fact, it's unseasonably cold and we have already begun to light the old, wood-fired stove. We have finished our wine making for another season with good results just in time for the return of Rebecca and Marcel, who will be staying for three weeks before they head back to New Zealand. Rebecca intends to swim across our bay every morning to get fit, but a week later the weather deteriorates as winter strikes unexpectedly. The rain continues and almost spoils the visit of Rebecca's three girlfriends from the United Kingdom. We huddle under tarpaulins as we grill lunch for our visitors and get wet and soggy walking with them around the village and to the beach at Vaja. Determined not to leave the village without a swim, the sisters, together with Rebecca and Marcel, all brave the cold sea at Vaja.

Shortly after the departure of all of our visitors olive harvest is upon us again. Sadly, it's a very poor olive harvest this season. For the second season in a row, firstly, it rained heavily when the flowers were setting and then the potential crop was completely ruined when the wind began to blow strongly. Almost everyone's trees have suffered especially those in exposed places and yields are substantially less than 50% of normal. As our olive harvest and tree pruning is finished for this year we have decided it's time for a short holiday. It couldn't be better timing when our friend Gorga telephones to invite us to visit her in Zagreb.

Almost as soon as we drive away from our village it starts to rain and within a short space of time it becomes torrential. Struggling to see out of the windscreen we begin to wonder if we will actually make it to the airport in Dubrovnik. As we drive on, the sky becomes so heavy and dark it's almost like night, even though it's only eleven o'clock in the morning! After a slow, nerve-racking journey, at last we reach the airport, only to find that everything is flooded. Denis' trousers and shoes get soaked in the knee deep flood water in the car park. Inside the new terminal there are buckets everywhere catching the water from numerous leaks in the roof! Fortunately, I remain warm and dry in my ankle length fur coat having been dropped off at the door. The flight to Zagreb is very short and as we descend there is a great view over the city. Most of the houses here are built from brick and plaster and have a distinctly Austrian influence with their sloping roofs to enable the snow to slide off during winter.

The temperature is much lower in Zagreb, but it's not an issue as Gorga's apartment in the suburb of Remete is well heated. Outside, it's not much more than zero degrees and although we find it cold, we are lucky as there is no rain for the duration of our visit. On our first excursion into the centre of the city we go for a walk to see the Christmas decorations which have just been put up. There are people everywhere. Many are shopping for Christmas presents; others are clustered in groups eating chestnuts roasted and sold by locals on many street corners from small mobile carts. The atmosphere is happy and relaxed and the decorations are so spectacular that I find it difficult to stop looking at them when it's time for dinner in the small, Italian restaurant that Gorga has chosen for us.

Gorga is working for the five days that we are staying with her so we are left to our own devices most of the time to explore the city. There is excellent shopping here with far more variety than in either Korčula or Dubrovnik and there are many beautiful, old churches, art galleries and of course the magnificent, sprawling Maksimir Park. We must be selective with the places we decide to visit as we just do not have sufficient time to see everything.

One of the most beautiful, old buildings we visit, which is close to Gorga's apartment in Remete is the particularly special Church of the Ascension of the Virgin Mary. Covering most of the walls and the ceiling are some of the most amazing frescoes I have ever seen. Most of them are complete having been restored by Gorga some years ago at the height of her career as a fresco restoration artist. The intricate detail and soft, pastel colours totally take my breath away.

On this visit to Zagreb we are hoping to be rewarded with some culture and we're incredibly pleased when one of Gorga's ballet dancer friends gives us tickets to the Nutcracker Suite in the National Theatre. It's a wonderful production with beautiful costumes and talented, fairy-tale dancing in a superb, old building. At the end of the evening we go for a drink in the Kavkaz Theatre café next door, which has been in existence since 1906. It's a fitting end to a thoroughly, enjoyable evening.

Gorga moved on from fresco restoration some time ago and today she takes us for coffee in a particularly, trendy cafe where she has painted designs on the walls. Once again her eye for detail is outstanding. There's a large mural of green leaves covering one wall and in a different area, gilded, abstract artwork. Her work is intricate and eye catching. She is clearly a very, talented artist.

Our time in Zagreb has been too short and allowed us to see only a few of the delights that this beautiful city has to offer and with promises to return in the not too distant future we fly back to Dubrovnik just as it begins to rain.

Upon our return to Račišće, we have a few days to get organised before the arrival of unexpected visitors just before Christmas. My cousin Geoffrey and his wife, Rebecca, who live close to New York, are coming for a long weekend. I'm particularly excited to catch up with Geoffrey as we have lost touch over the years. I think I was probably about twelve when I last saw him and, of course, I have never met his wife. My cousin is so delightfully laid back he's almost falling over and Rebecca and I hit it off immediately. She teaches English at a university in the USA and arrives with a huge pile of novels for me. Unfortunately, it rains for the whole weekend. However, we have plenty to talk about; family; books and a catch up of our respective lives. Geoffrey quickly becomes addicted to Denis' espresso, which he names 'Fru Fru' coffee, and also Denis' wine.

Trapped indoors by the weather, we all eat and drink far too much as we relax in the warmth radiating from our old wood-burning stove. Nothing detracts from the good time we're all having, not even walking around Korčula with Geoffrey and Rebecca trying to take photographs in the pouring rain!

Winter is well and truly here by Christmas and the village is now extremely quiet. The figs and pomegranates that line the path behind our house are bare; nothing more than brown sticks reaching towards the sky; so different from their green, summer state. As I continue on down to the village there is no one about. Most people are indoors and keep to themselves. The sea is sombre grey; a reflection of the sky and all the small boats are quiet, still and empty. There are not even any fishermen out today braving the winter weather. Venturing around to the other side of the bay I come to a large plaque on the wall of one of the houses. It commemorates six, local men who were lined up against a stone wall and executed by German soldiers in 1943. Their bodies were dumped into the sea where they remained for four days as, fearing that they too would be shot, no one had the courage to pull them out.

On my walk home the only person I come across is an old baba rugged-up against the winter cold in layers of black clothing and thick black stockings. In the middle of winter it's dark by five-thirty at night and not light until eight in the morning. Today, it's particularly cold and I'm sure it will be early to bed tonight with my electric blanket and a good book.

The only invitation we receive is from Pavo and his family to share the traditional, Croatian Christmas Eve meal of bakalar, a simple, smoked cod and potato stew. Unfortunately, Pavo's wife has not taken enough care with the preparation of the meal and what should be a tasty, flavoursome stew, turns out to be a mouthful of oily, salty bones! Pavo shakes his head after the first couple of mouthfuls and says, "This is no good. My wife she is lazy!"

On Christmas Day it's just the two of us and a superb piece of roast pork with all the trimmings, including our own new potatoes, freshly dug from the garden. It's a very quiet Christmas, but at least the midday meal, which includes traditional kroštule for dessert, is particularly tasty. After Christmas, the heavy winter rain is constant and we are beginning to feel trapped within the confines of our house. No one is outside working the land. Even when there is a break in the weather and Denis goes out to work in one of our olive groves the locals with their depressive winter attitudes, stare at him from the doorways of their house as if he is peculiar. The store is only open for three hours in the morning and two hours in the evening. The hotel and Konoba Vala are both closed and the bocce court is deserted. Korčula too is a ghost town. We can only find one café open and it has no food for sale in winter. The banks and a couple of hardware shops are the only businesses operating, everything else is closed. All I can think about is our upcoming escape to Paris for ten days on 7 February.

By the time we get to Paris we are both like a couple of wild animals who have been released from their cages. What bliss; ten days of shopping, eating, drinking (particularly champagne and oysters) and trips to various interesting venues. It's snowing lightly most of the time, but somehow the snow seems romantic and makes wandering around my favourite European city, soaking up the sights and sounds, even more enjoyable. For me the highlights of this trip are definitely the Musée de Cluny where I am stunned by the absolutely, magnificent, intricate, mediaeval tapestries and the Musée d'Orsay where there are so many fine works by the Impressionists. When it begins to rain on our last morning in Paris, I know it must be time to go home.

Apparently, during our stay in Paris we were fortunate enough to miss several more days of even heavier rain in Račišće. The month of February is not over yet, but the rainfall is already well in excess of the usual amount. We are beginning to wonder if the rainy season will ever stop and if we really want to spend next winter in Račišće.

Recipes

Bakalar (Croatian Cod Stew)

500 gm dried salted cod
1 kg diced potatoes
1 large onion finely chopped
4 cloves of garlic, chopped
chopped parsley
olive oil
salt and pepper

Wash cod and soak overnight in water. Wash again and cover with fresh water and cook slowly on low heat until tender – about 4 hours. Remove cod from the water and reserve water. Carefully remove the bones. Sauté onion, garlic and parsley in olive oil then add potatoes and stir until coated with oil. Add the reserved water and cook until potatoes are tender, then return the cod to the pot. Simmer slowly for 20 minutes. Season with salt and pepper and serve with crusty bread.

Kroštule (Bowknots)

500 gm plain flour
2 tsp baking powder
good pinch of salt
2 eggs
50 gm sugar
50 gm melted butter
1 tbsp (or more to taste) rakija or rum
grated rind of a lemon/orange
100 ml milk
sunflower oil for frying
icing sugar to dust

Sift flour, baking powder and salt into a bowl. In another bowl, beat eggs and sugar until light and foamy. Add the butter, rakija, lemon and orange rind. Stir the egg mixture into the flour and mix with a wooden spoon to form a dough. Mix in enough milk to make a soft dough. On a lightly floured surface knead the dough for 5 minutes. Put in a bowl and cover with a tea towel and leave it to rise for 30 minutes. Turn the dough out and break into 6 pieces. Roll and cut into thin strips about 1.5 × 10 cm. Tie each strip into a knot or bow. Fry in hot oil a few at a time until golden brown. Drain on kitchen paper and dust with icing sugar.

23
More Trouble in Paradise

It's now close to a year since I applied to change my name in Croatia and when at last I finally receive an update from my lawyer it seems that there are problems. Just less than a year ago all the necessary papers to register my birth and my marriage were sent to the registrar in Korčula; however, he did not respond. When my lawyer did not hear from him, he began ringing him repeatedly. Sometimes, the registrar would purposely cut him off as soon as he said who he was and what he was calling about. At other times he'd say he'd call him back, but he never did. His most appalling piece of behaviour was to answer the telephone giving a false name and when the lawyer asked to speak to the registrar, he said that 'he' was out! After making about thirty calls, the lawyer has now given up and he is suggesting that I go to see the registrar myself, armed with copies of my documents.

I encountered the registrar a couple of years ago when I was making enquiries about my family tree and after that particular experience I am expecting him to be surly and antagonistic and unsurprisingly I am reluctant to face him. After thinking about the matter for a few days, I decide to enlist the help of the Korčula police inspector whom I've spoken to recently in relation to Denis' temporary stay permit. The inspector said I could call him if I needed any help, so I've accepted his offer. After I brief him, the inspector contacts the registrar and discovers that although he has done work on my file, what he's done is actually laughable.

Nine months ago the registrar accepted that my previous marriage had been legally dissolved, but then he changed his mind. When the inspector asked him what made him have a change of heart, he said that it was his prerogative to do as he pleased without having to give anyone an explanation! He then took it upon himself to write, without my permission; to my ex-husband of twenty years ago, asking him to confirm that our marriage had actually ended! His non-airmail letter was written in Croatian and posted to a New Zealand address that was more than twenty years old! His letter came back to his office last week; nine months after he'd originally posted it, and was marked 'gone no address!' Totally astounded at the registrar's stupidity, the inspector succeeded in convincing him that it was now time to move on and register my current marriage. Hoping that the registrar will now be more reasonable, I go to see him.

It does not surprise me, when I confront the registrar, that he emphatically denies having received either my papers or any phone calls from my lawyer! Now, as I sit in his office waiting, he is finally attending to my registration. Of course, he's angry that I called the police inspector so he is working as slowly as he possibly can. He cannot hide the look of irritation that clouds his face and perhaps this is deliberate. The registration is, in fact, a two-minute job, but he turns it into a fifteen-minute one by staring at his office walls constantly and when his eyes alight on one of his posters he stops work and becomes fixated. They are an odd assortment, his wall coverings. There's a poster of the now deceased Pope and the current Pope; his favourite football team and a huge elaborate wine calendar. Finally, his printer spits out my completed marriage registration.

"You must pay now, forty kuna." His voice is sour and unpleasant. I hand him a hundred kuna note, which he puts in his drawer before shutting it and declaring with a smile that he has no change! He's ripped me off, but I don't care, after a year of waiting, at last this piece of paperwork is finished.

"I'm very happy, thank you," I smile or perhaps it's more of a grimace.

"I am happy, too," he says smiling broadly. "My first name is Zadovoljan. You know that in English it means happy!"

We hadn't given any thought to the renewal of Denis' temporary stay permit until I was in the police station with regard to papers I needed for the registrar and we bumped into the officious woman who deals with Denis' file. She asked us to wait while she produced a lengthy, unreasonable complicated list of requirements for Denis to produce before applying to renew his TSP. His existing TSP doesn't actually expire until 1 April, which is six weeks away, but as the list is so large Denis decides to begin assembling the papers straightaway hoping to avoid any possible problems. The task is not easy and proves to be very time consuming. He needs letters from the court stating that he has no criminal convictions or any debts; the confirmed renewal of his compulsory health insurance; a letter from the bank stating that he has sufficient money on which to live; the registration of our marriage; and new copies of all my papers. The last request is completely ridiculous as there has been no change in either of our circumstances and most of these documents must come from either New Zealand, where we were both born, or Australia, where we were married, at a considerable cost and with lengthy delays.

Sometime later, when Denis has collected all the new papers on the list he presents himself, once again at the police station. Foolishly, we are expecting the usual overbearing woman dealing with his application to be pleased with his efficiency, but she is not. With a frosty, superior look on her face, she begins to try and intimidate Denis. We are both rather surprised by her attitude. She is actually a slim, attractive woman somewhere in her mid-thirties with long, brown hair and when we first met her we had no idea she would be such a dragon as her appearance and her personality just don't seem to go together at all.

"The rules have changed and you do not have all the necessary documents. One important one is missing." Needless to say this document has never been mentioned before and it is not on the list. She continues with her bully tactics and lectures him.

"This is procedure and you must learn to do as you are told without asking questions!" She says before telling him that now he must enter into an agreement to rent a room in our house from me! If it wasn't all so deadly serious I might actually find this whole scenario funny, Denis, however, does not. It proves too much for him and he explodes causing Mrs Officious to turn into a stone wall and give him yet another lecture. Livid with rage, he comes to the obvious conclusion that new rules are invented constantly just to ensure that things are as difficult as possible for the applicant. We begin to wonder if this country is still being run by Communists when the bully utters her final insult.

"If I decline your application when I process it, then I will send you a registered letter demanding that you present yourself in my office within fifteen days to give me an explanation!" We simply cannot believe the words that have been spat out of her mouth. As we depart the police station in shock, we know that we have just encountered a particularly, virulent weed with a giant, tap root that is deeply embedded in the system. What are the chances of uprooting her, we wonder?

The rental agreement has too many large, technical, Croatian words in it and we need Pavo's help to complete it. Over a glass of wine, Denis and Pavo study it. Clearly, Pavo is nervous and reluctant to help Denis fill it in and I realise that his mindset is typical of many of the locals. It seems that many people here will blindly do whatever they are told without question as they are completely terrified of authority. We have no doubt that this is yet another hangover from the Communist era.

Having filled in the agreement we are now sure that this must be the last possible piece of paper work; however, when Denis returns to the Police Station the bully has managed to find yet another stumbling block. Denis' passport, which is still current, isn't new enough for her and she insists that he apply for another one from the New Zealand Internal Affairs office in London!

At about this time, Denis is summoned to see the police inspector regarding his application for Croatian citizenship which he'd filed in Auckland almost a year ago. The inspector and the bully have been instructed to interview Denis by the higher authority in Zagreb. Most of the interview is routine. The inspector comments on the fact that Denis lives in Croatia with me, his Croatian wife and compliments him on his use of the Croatian language. Then, of course, there are the usual questions such as, "Are you a member of any subversive political parties? Have you ever been in trouble with the police either here or in New Zealand?" Near the end of the interview, when it seems as if he definitely has a good grasp of Denis' situation, he suddenly says, "So why are you applying for citizenship now? You know, of course, that it's a waste of time, don't you?" His tone is not actually rude. He just seems rather perplexed.

"No I don't. I'm applying on advice from both my lawyer in Dubrovnik and also the Croatian consul in New Zealand, on the grounds of reunification of family as my wife is a Croatian citizen," Denis replies, shocked by what he's just heard. The inspector and the bully both stare blankly at Denis.

"But you're not eligible for citizenship for at least another five years!" Continues the inspector.

"That's not what I've been told by either my lawyer or the Croatian consul." Yet again Denis can't believe what they are saying and little does he realise there's more to come.

"Huh!" Says the bully. "Lawyers and consular people don't know what they're doing. They don't understand the rules and they're incompetent!"

Denis departs feeling rather dejected to say the least. The entire bureaucratic process here is beginning to turn into our worst nightmare. We have never been treated as rudely as this before and as we are not yet finished with this drama, there may be more unpleasant surprises to come. Quite frankly, it is spoiling our existence in paradise.

Denis' new passport takes so long to arrive from London (over a month) that we are beginning to think there is a problem; however, the only problem is with the Croatian postal system. When the post office here quote you a time frame for delivery, the reality is that it usually takes twice as long as they say it will. Finally, his new passport leaves London by courier and arrives in Split, but we are exasperated even further when a woman rings to say that they don't courier mail to the islands!

A few days later, I'm writing in my office when the phone rings. It's the bully from the police station calling to inform us that Denis has been granted Croatian citizenship. Does she congratulate him and is she pleased for him? No! All she can say is,

"I don't know how you got this. You must know someone in Zagreb!" Is she actually accusing him of bribery?!

Day by day, my stress levels are increasing, I simply can't believe the ridiculous bureaucratic nonsense we are encountering here. Hoping to temporarily blot it out, every day I walk to the beach at Vaja in the late afternoon spring sunshine. As I leave the house, via the back path, the fig and pomegranate trees are covered with new leaves. After the bleak days of winter, the green fig and the rusty, red, pomegranate leaves seem vivid. Our lilac tree has already begun to flower and today, it's surrounded by a cloud of large, lemon-yellow butterflies. I've never had a lilac in my garden before and although it flowers very early in spring and the blooms don't last very long, it's an exceptionally, pretty tree with a lovely fragrance.

Closer to Vaja, the sides of the road are a profusion of beautiful, spring flowers; pink, white and purple daises, yellow and pink snapdragons, the tiniest, bright, pink cyclamen I have ever seen and purple and white irises. The wild flowers here are numerous. It's simply stunning. I can't help but wonder if the people here appreciate it. As the earth is covered with flowers so the sky is filled with birds. Spring is nesting time for the swallows. All day long, they are busy darting in and out of the house eaves carrying straw and nest building materials. Up close, they are iridescent, dark blue and turquoise and quite lovely.

Walking back to the village from Vaja, the vegetation beyond the roadside is thick and dense. There are many olives and also numerous fig trees here. Looking at the tiny figs as they begin to form I wonder if the Garden of Eden looked as beautiful as this. Almond trees with slender branches and long leaves are covered with furry, pale green fruit. Many of the locals claim to love eating them now, before they are really ready for picking. When I bite into their sour, crunchy, greenness, thinking that maybe one day I will acquire a taste for them, I wonder with everything that is happening here at the moment, if perhaps I am eating the forbidden fruit in the Garden of Eden.

Now, is also the season for wild asparagus, if you know where to look for it. We have been given a bunch by a friendly old lady who knows all the spots where it is found and we are looking forward to tasting it. Thinner and longer than the cultivated variety, sadly it's so bitter and nasty tasting that we rate it inedible! It will definitely not be added to our list of culinary delights.

Today, it's raining and much too wet to contemplate a walk. Instead I must return to my bureaucratic war. Another visit to my enemy the registrar is on my calendar. Although he has registered my marriage I have just found out that he has not registered my birth. Our car is parked at the top of the path behind our house and when we go to get in, to drive to Korčula, two of the tyres are flat and it looks as if someone has punctured them intentionally. Ranko comes to the rescue and gives Denis a lift to the garage to get them repaired. The tyre man confirms our conclusion and says to Denis,

"Someone has punctured your tyres with a very sharp object such as a needle. So what did you do? Screw your neighbour's wife or park in his garage!"

At least his sense of humour lightens the situation a little. We are beginning to think we are being picked on until a week later when three of Ranko's tyres suffer the same fate. During the next few days, this small incident is the talk of the village. However, no one will own up to the crime and we are told that the naughty boys in the village get up to no good late on Saturday nights.

Our tyres have been repaired and our car is now mobile and it's time to see the registrar yet again. This time, when I enter his office and state my business, he looks guilty. Today, I have purposely not brought along any documents with me as I know that they have already been sent to him some time ago and this time I intend to insist that he finds them. As soon as I arrive, he suggests immediately that I go away and come back later, but I refuse telling him I prefer to wait. He stares at me coldly for some moments before he begins to make a show of searching his desk, pretending to look for my documents. Of course, there is nothing to be found so he then sits nervously twiddling his thumbs while I stare at him intensely without blinking. In the end, when he has no other option he opens his 'hard basket;' the bottom left drawer of his desk. The 'hard basket' is an extremely big, fat, file full to overflowing with documents that he has obviously not attended to. When he can no longer cope with me watching him he blurts out,

"It was my leg, I couldn't work last year!"

Watching him work, I wonder how many other people are waiting in vain for their registrations to be actioned. Judging by the size of his file, I would say dozens. Today, he knows that I have his measure and he is somewhat contrite when I pay. As I leave his office, hopefully for the last time, I wonder what he is actually paid to do and why they continue to employ such an incompetent fool.

The frustrating process to change my name continues. My application has now been referred by my lawyer to a different worker in the office upstairs from Zadovoljan. When he receives my application, this sour bureaucrat rings me asking for extra, unnecessary documents. Once again, it's clearly a tactic he has invented to delay the process even further. Denis just happens to be in Korčula when the new bureaucrat calls and we decide that it would be a good idea for Denis to clarify his superfluous request. Sourpuss, as we've named him, turns out to be even more obstructive than Zadovoljan.

"So your wife wants her name changed, does she?" Sourpuss says in a voice dripping with sarcasm.

"Yes!" Replies Denis. "She was born Unković and she wants to die Unković!" Sourpuss is not expecting this answer and when he cannot come up with a response he turns on Denis demanding to know about *his* citizenship, which is, of course, totally irrelevant.

Two months later, Sourpuss has still not done anything to change my name. A call to my lawyer ascertains that if he has still not completed the process at the end of sixty days then we must report him to his superiors. What is wrong with these people? Why do they have such malicious, obstructive attitudes?

Things seem to have settled down a little with our paperwork war and just when we are beginning to be hopeful that the worst is over, the postman delivers a blue envelope to me. Here, these seldom contain good news and this one is no exception.

For some months we have been asking each other why I have not received the monthly returns that customs promised to send me to complete in relation to our coffee beans. We had come to the conclusion that customs must no longer require returns when, suddenly, the blue envelope with a registered letter inside, arrives. It seems that they want to fine me for not furnishing returns. Their notice, which I pass onto my lawyer, gives me eight days in which to appeal a fine of eighteen thousand kuna or $4,600NZD. My lawyer speaks to them briefly and asks why they did not send me the returns to complete and they tell him that they were not obliged to! We have heard from other sources that customs are trying to extort money from foreigners in any way they can as the country is broke and I have no doubt that what they are attempting to do to me proves that what we have heard is obviously true. My lawyer files the appeal and now we must wait for a response from customs, which, apparently, will take months. As far as we can see there isn't much more trouble that we could possibly encounter here in paradise, however, once again, we are wrong.

As part of the registration of my birth and marriage here, I was obliged to show proof of residence in Croatia. To do this I used a copy of the title for our property. The land registration system here is antiquated and mediaeval. It took in excess of two years for my name to be put on the title and when we finally get updated copies of these from the land registry office we are shocked. There are three other names incorrectly recorded on my titles! Apparently there are no simple paperwork procedures here and we are not surprised when our lawyer asks us to go to the Katastar in Korčula and take photos of the pages in the land registers. He will study them and hopefully find out how these people got on the title of my property.

After checking out the land registry documents our lawyer ascertains that the problem has been caused by the previous owner from whom I purchased our property. He was too lazy to complete the appropriate registrations in respect of the sale correctly and consequently other parties have been able to register claims of ownership against our property. My lawyer has now written to him asking him to correct his oversight immediately. However, we both doubt that he will do anything as he no longer owns the properties and if he couldn't be bothered to do it when he sold them, then why would he be bothered to do it now? We have no choice but to leave this problem in our lawyer's hands hoping he can fix it as soon as possible. However, knowing this country as we do now, we doubt very much that this can be fixed with any haste.

Clare comes to visit just after we have found out about the problems with the title on our property and when I relate them to her she doesn't seem at all surprised and responds with,

"Well perhaps I should tell you about the title for our house. It's taken me three different lawyers and nine years to finally get it into our name! I wish you luck sorting yours out quicker than we did. And, by the way, you know about the land registry office don't you?" She asks.

"No, I don't. Tell me!"

"Well," She says. "We've heard from more than one person that someone in there accepts money in return for putting names that don't legally belong onto titles of properties." Hearing that made me feel positively sick and I knew I could do nothing more than place my hope and faith in my lawyer.

24
The Garden of Eden

As time passes and we continue to live in the time warp that envelopes this old village, we know that in the quest to trace my family tree we have happened upon natural, mostly unspoilt beauty and peace. This probably isn't surprising as the entire island is dotted with fig trees, which are known to be a symbol of abundance, fertility and sweetness. However, sometimes things are not quite as they seem.

After ten years here, our Australian friends, Tom and Clare, have listed their house for sale and will be returning to Australia. They tell us that, the small village mentality has finally done them in. They believe that even though Tom has immediate family here, they have not been accepted and the highly successful bed and breakfast business that Clare has established has been greeted by the locals with nothing but jealousy and scorn. The German couple will also be getting on their bikes and cycling away. They, too, have struggled to gain acceptance in Račišće and feel unwelcome. What would my father have thought of his homeland today, I wonder? Would he have been content living in the Garden of Eden or would the corrupt bureaucracy and old, die-hard, Communistic ways have unsettled him as they have me?

Croatia has applied to join the European Union and hopes to do so in 2013. When we mention this to the locals they close their minds to it and the most common reaction is,

"Europe's finished, gone to the dogs. What do we want to be part of that for?"

If and when it becomes a member, what will happen to my idyllic island of Korčula? There are many people here who do not want to be part of the EU, particularly the older ones, but also a surprising number of the young ones. They know it is inevitable that the cost of living will rise substantially once the euro arrives, and they also fear that Europeans will buy up their properties and totally change the face of the village. EU membership also means the loss of state subsidies and in this village this will mean that the locals will no longer be paid a subsidy to press their olive oil.

On a national scale, many of the country's civil servants are worried that they will become unemployed as their performances are not up to the standards required by the EU. Once they lose their jobs, they believe that they will be replaced by Europeans who are more qualified, hard working and enterprising. Large numbers of government workers are at present just biding their time waiting for the payoffs that they know their unions will be insisting upon. One of the main conditions for Croatia to join the EU is the stamping out of corruption and soft jobs, which hopefully will mean that bribery and fraud will no longer have a place here. Once this finally happens, people like Zadovoljan and Sourpuss will surely be unemployed.

Recently Croatia's new President apologised publicly to Bosnia Herzegovina and Serbia for Croatia's aggression during the war. He has begun to bury the hatchet, as he strives to gain acceptance for his country as a member of the EU. Most of the population were outraged by his behaviour and felt that he was being disloyal to his people. There was even talk of impeachment. It seems that I am surrounded by ostriches with their heads buried in the sand. Should we stay or should we go? Sadly, it seems that after tasting and enjoying Croatia's forbidden fruit until we completely gorged ourselves, that we, too, must now leave the Garden of Eden.